A BRAND
TO DIE FOR

A L E X P E A R L

Fizgig Press
London

A CIP catalogue record for this book is available from
the British Library.

ISBN 979-8-8315-2690-5

Typeset by Abdul Rehman
Cover design by Alejandro Baigorri

For David,
without whom this book wouldn't
have seen the light of day.
I am happy that all errors are attributed to him.

Q:
"Good to see you Mr Bond. Things have been awfully dull around here...
I hope we're going to have some gratuitous sex and violence."

James Bond:
"I certainly hope so too."

Never Say Never Again 1983

PROLOGUE

————— ··●·· —————

It was one of those fucking awful grey, damp and bitterly cold days in June that England was so good at. Angus Lovejoy didn't want to be here. Obviously. Who'd choose to be at a funeral for someone you'd never known - personally, that is? Of course, he knew who Danny Deedes had been. He'd been the Deedes of *Gordon Deedes Rutter*, the ad agency he now found himself working at. Well, the word 'working' may have been pushing it a tad. He'd been here for a month now and still hadn't received a sodding creative brief. Not that he was complaining.

If truth be known, he'd been a bitter disappointment to his parents. They had had high hopes for him. They had set their sights on the Foreign Office. But it all started going horribly wrong when he'd been sent down from Charterhouse for shagging the Chancellor's daughter in the cricket pavilion.

Still, as far as he was concerned, he envisaged a reasonably bright future for himself in the advertising game. GDR was, after all, one of London's most creative hot shops and its creative director Magnus O'Shea had loved his portfolio of TV scripts and press ads.

The agency had been informed of Danny Deedes's premature demise no more than a week ago. It was Dick his chauffeur who had broken the news. Dick was a lovely man who had been affectionately known by one and all as 'Danny's Dick'. Danny, needless to say, had been gay, flamboyant and about as promiscuous as it was possible to be. He'd made his name in the 50s as a TV producer when commercial television was just starting out and had single-handedly set up one of London's first commercial production companies. On the back of this early success, he'd then gone on to set up his own advertising agency and was eventually bought out on very amicable and favourable terms by the current partners. In fact, he had even retained an office in the building from which he apparently wrote TV commercials for his own client, some large partwork magazine publisher. The strange thing was that Danny Deedes may have been a clever sod with a certain charm and twinkle in the eye, but according to everyone who knew him, he didn't possess a single creative bone in his body, and the commercials he penned for his client were something of an embarrassment to the agency. Indeed, the management never knowingly advertised the fact.

The vicar had finished his short address and had now gesticulated to an old boy in a morning suit and tails who stumbled forward to the dais and coughed and spluttered into the microphone.

'Today is a very sad day... My name is Bernard Smythe-Rodney, and I knew Danny way back in the 50s when we worked together producing TV commercials for the likes of Player's Cigarettes and Johnny Walker... Those were the days... What a lovely man he was... Salt of the earth... They just don't make them like that anymore...'

Angus was sitting next to a man in a trench coat that he'd spoken to earlier. He'd been the agency's first creative director, and now the man was discreetly leaning forward and whispering into Angus's ear.

'Funny that... I always thought he was a bit of a shit.'

CHAPTER ONE

The office on the corner of Great Pulteney Street, Soho was a terrific location for any self-respecting creative advertising agency that prided itself on producing innovative, award-winning campaigns.

Soho was a seething hotbed of creativity. Between the seedy sex shops and massage parlours, ad agencies rubbed shoulders with production companies, recording studios, illustration studios, editing suites, and publishing houses. And after working hours, the bars and bistros were full to the gunwales with creative types and celebrities from the world of showbiz.

It was clearly the place to be seen.

Unfortunately for Gordon Deedes Rutter, Paddy O'Leary and Sean Flaherty also thought it was a good place to park themselves. And the precise location in Soho that they favoured was the large red-tiled doorstep on the corner of Pulteney Street with its fancy glass doors.

Soho had its fair share of vagrants and door sleepers and Paddy and Sean were very much part of that community.

When Magnus had parked his BMW in the NCP car park, he made his way to the office and could almost smell Paddy and Sean before feasting his eyes on the pair. They were perched on the doorstep with a bottle of cheap Frascati with a plastic basket moulded to the glass. Through bleary eyes, Paddy waved the bottle at Magnus. 'Best of the morning to yer.'

Magnus tried hard not to retch. 'Look, fellas. I know you like this spot, but how would you like to earn yourselves 50 quid?'

The pair looked at him with incredulity as Magnus pulled five crisp ten-pound notes from his wallet. 'All I'm asking is that you go down the road and sit on the doorstep of the other corner building at the end of the street. You can't miss it. There's a big logo on the door that reads *RHB*. I can vouch for them. They are extremely nice people. And to be honest, they have a much nicer entrance than we do.'

Paddy snatched the notes and the two reluctantly rose from the step and swayed down the road to their new home.

RHB was, of course, an arch-rival of Gordon Deedes Rutter's, and was irritatingly doing rather well, having picked up a long succession of impressive clients in recent months including a relatively new German car manufacturer and the world's largest manufacturer of jeans.

Magnus smiled to himself as he stepped into the lobby and was greeted by Nicola, the agency's new receptionist. He had a busy morning and was in need of a strong black coffee. The previous day's funeral in Highgate had been a pretty surreal affair. And seeing all those characters from the past was a bit like going to an old school reunion. Everyone still had the same voices and mannerisms but in most cases were barely recognisable.

Part of him still felt the odd pang of guilt over buying Danny out of his own agency. But to be fair, they had behaved honourably. They'd left his name on the door and his office on the first floor remained his. And they had turned a blind eye to the shit he produced for Marshall Cavendish. For

Christ's sake, they had even kept Danny's Dick on the payroll.

He switched on the TV to look at the news headlines. It was part of his daily routine. He didn't know why. The news was always so bloody depressing.

'Our opinion poll shows that the Tories are increasing their lead over Labour... there is no doubt that this is the Tories' election. We asked thousands of voters across the country what factor was putting the Conservatives ahead. Was it because of the experienced ministerial team; the policies; or Mrs Thatcher's leadership? Experienced ministers said 11%. Conservative policies said 31%. But a majority 46% said that it was down to Mrs Thatcher's leadership. Yesterday that leadership came under bitter attack from Dennis Healey who accused her of glorying in slaughter. The same day we asked whether the Falklands factor was helping or hindering the government's chances of winning. Making no difference said 37%. Hindering said 13%. But helping said 44%. And it's that majority that Labour is now trying to assault.'

He flicked the TV off with his remote. 'Of course, it's bloody helping her... There's nothing like a sodding war and a bit of flag-waving to get the electorate fired up. And that bitch knows it well enough...'

Penny, his creative secretary, entered with his coffee.

'Are you being rude about our Prime Minister?'

'Would I do such a thing?' He wasn't expecting an answer. 'You're a star, hon... What would I do without you?'

'Make it yourself I s'pose.' She placed the mug on his desk and opened his ostentatious leather diary. 'You have a busy day, today.'

'Yeah. Talk me through it.'

'Well, in about five minutes you are interviewing an art director by the name of Brian Finkle to work with the lovely Angus. Then at 10.00, you have a meeting with Robert and Martin about the forthcoming pitch for Olivetti. At 2.00 you're reviewing all the new work for the Solid Fuel Advisory Service. At 4.00 Stella and Alistair have a meeting booked with you to go through the first round of creative work for the new fizzy drink Quatro. And then at 5.30, it's the speech to the nation and Kenneth wants you to give us all an update on the work front and what's going through production. Oh, and when you get a spare moment, which you probably won't, you need to check through all the entries for the Cannes Awards and sign all the entries. All the work has been mounted with all the right labels. I think poor Steve had a nervous breakdown putting it together last Friday. It's all got to go off by the end of this week otherwise we're going to miss the deadline.'

Magnus plonked himself on the big leather sofa and sipped at his coffee, while Penny busied herself by watering the newly installed cactus and Yucca plant by the window. As she did so, his phone rang. It was reception. Mr Finkle had arrived to see him.

'Thanks, Nicola. Do you want to send him up?'

Magnus cleared the detritus from the glass table and while chucking an empty Stella Artois bottle into his bin, there came a tapping on his open door.

'Ah, do come in. It's Brian, isn't it?'

'Yes... I'm a bit early... Hope that's alright.' Brian certainly looked the part. Lots of designer stubble, tortoiseshell framed glasses and a duffel coat. If he were auditioning for the part of an art director at an ad agency, he'd have bagged the part and the wardrobe department would have been out of a job.

'No, that's absolutely fine. It makes a refreshing change for anyone to be on time, let alone early, at this place. Come and take a seat. Can I get you a coffee?'

'Thanks. Black without sugar would be great.'

Magnus lifted his phone. 'Hi, Pen. Can I trouble you for a black coffee and no sugar, hon?'

'You didn't have to call. I sit outside your office, remember?'

Magnus smiled and put the receiver down. It was a fair point. But the thing was, he liked playing the part of Creative Director, and he liked Penny doing everything for him. She was bloody good at it, and in truth, she quite liked doing it. He made her laugh and she did stuff for him. It was a fair trade-off.

'Do you want to put your book on the table?'

Brian opened his portfolio. And Magnus remembered it instantly. He'd liked it when he first had it sent over by the headhunters. He didn't have to see it again. He'd already decided to hire him. He was the best art director he'd seen in a long while. He was a lot better than half the department in terms of the standard of design and the quality of his thinking. It was astonishing that nobody had already snapped him up.

'So remind me... Where were you before? And how many other agencies are you talking to?'

Brian smiled. 'Oh, I'm from St. Martins... the art college. And you are the first and only agency I've spoken to so far.'

Magnus nodded. *Shit... Fuck... Magnus old boy. This is your lucky fucking day. Just act cool... Hang on, no. Don't do that you twat. If you don't tell him you want him, he'll fuck off down the road and get hired by those tossers with the tramps in their doorway.*

'Look Brian. I'm going to be really honest with you... '

Brian's palms went all sweaty. *This guy hated his stuff. He could tell. He probably thought it was too off the wall. Amateurish. Badly art directed...*

17

'I think your work is... bloody amazing... I absolutely love it... Would you consider working here for us?'

There was a palpable silence. Brian couldn't believe it. He was sitting in one of the best creative agencies in town. It was top of his hit list. He'd have worked here for bloody nothing just to get his feet under a desk. He could hardly believe what he was hearing.

'Well... er...'

'Look, I tell you what. If you accept today, I can promise you an exceptional package... 18K, company car... private medical insurance, pension benefits... What do you say?

'The only downside is that you'll be working with a bit of a wanker... No, I'm joking... He's a perfectly nice guy. But just don't tell him what you're earning, because it may go down like a shit sandwich... And creative teams are a bit like marriages... But look at it this way: in the fullness of time, if it all works out with you two, the agency will match his remuneration with yours. What do you say, Brian?'

18K? That was insane. 'Yeah... that sounds great. I'd love to accept your offer, Mr O'Shea.'

'Oh, just call me Magnus... We're very informal here... Some people just call me Dickhead... Look, while you're here, let me introduce you to Angus, your copywriter. He sits further down the corridor.'

CHAPTER TWO

— ·•●•· —

Angus always kept his door closed. He didn't like to be disturbed when reading. He was on the last few pages of the new bestseller, *The Name of the Rose* by Umberto Eco.

He knew straight away that it would be Magnus. He was the only one in this place who never knocked. He didn't feel guilty about reading. After all, Magnus had told him to read in the first place if he didn't have anything to do. In fact, it was Magnus's bloody book. 'Just catch up on books, films and theatre if you don't have any work on. It's all relevant.' That's what he had said to him. And it kind of made sense in a funny kind of way.

Magnus popped his head round the door. 'How's the book?'

'Bloody brilliant. This guy can write can't he?'

'Tell me about it. I thought you'd like it... Look, I've got some really good news... You have an art director. Not any old art director, but a fucking brilliant one. Let me introduce you to Brian Finkle.'

Brian's designer-stubbled and bespectacled face appeared from the side of the door.

'Hi, it's great to meet you, Angus. I'm Brian. Brian Finkle.'

Angus smiled. 'Mr Finkle... That's a great name. Hope you're not fickle... My family name is Lovejoy. And yes, I suppose I am partial to a bit of joy... particularly if it involves shagging I suppose. When are you starting?'

'Bloody good question. We hadn't agreed that had we, Brian?'

'I can start whenever you'd like me to.'

'Fab. Let's say next Monday, as the finance director has to get the contract to you, which you'll need to sign and return. It'll take a couple of days. You can just bring it in with you on Monday.'

'You can have this window seat if you like, Brian. Probably best for the art director to sit by God's lightbox. And besides, you'll get a good view of the local nympho who strips off every Thursday at lunchtime.'

'Really?' Magnus looked a bit hurt. 'Nobody told me about that. Are you serious?'

'Course I am. Why do you think that animal Trevor has a telescope set up on a tripod next door?'

Magnus scratched his chin. 'I thought he was into bird watching.'

'Yeah, he is, but not the feathered variety.'

There was a spontaneous burst of laughter. And then Magnus pulled the door closed and started speaking in hushed tones.

'Actually, there's something I need to tell you about the animal next door. The agency is letting him go... Apparently, he's been fiddling his expenses for over a year and has admitted to stealing office furniture.'

Angus raised his eyebrows in disbelief. 'You're kidding... What kind of office furniture?'

'A boardroom table and six chairs.'

'Fuck my old boots.'

'Yeah. it's a pain in the arse. Because he's a bloody good art director and the Guinness client loves him to bits... thinks the sun shines out of his proverbial.'

'How did he get found out?'

'The idiot only went and put in expenses for a removal lorry down to fucking Brighton.'

'No...'

'Yeah... Couldn't make this stuff up if you tried, could you?'

'If he's on his bike, I might just nab that telescope.'

'Yeah... I would if I were you. He's on a shoot all day... Then, when he's gone we can all have a go at bird watching. Thursday lunchtimes you reckon?'

'Yeah. Lovely display. Regular as clockwork.'

CHAPTER THREE

— ·· ● ·· —

As an only child of left-wing Jewish parents, Brian had finally moved out of the family home almost six months ago. Had he stayed there any longer, he might well have murdered both of them in their sleep. The thought reminded him of that famous definition of the Yiddish word chutzpah by the Jewish author Leo Rosten. 'Chutzpah' he had written can be defined by the actions of the son who murders his parents and then claims mercy from the court on grounds of being an orphan... That's chutzpah.

His parents weren't especially religious, but like all Jewish parents, they possessed that peculiar Jewish gene. You know, the one - the Jewish obsessive-compulsive disorder one that meant they couldn't stop themselves from picking up the phone and ringing him every two minutes.

'Brian, tell me. How's the flat?'

'It's not a flat, mum. It's a room. And it's... Well, it's small.'

'I hope it's clean... You know you can get terrible things in small flats? Laurence's boy had cockroaches. Can you imagine? They had to get the environmental health people down. And then they discovered black mould... And black mould is the worst. It can kill you...'

'No, I don't have any black mould mum. It's very clean. Well, cleanish... And you'll be pleased to know that I haven't seen any cockroaches.'

'Of course, you haven't seen any cockroaches. They only come out at night... Anyway, I hope you're eating properly...'

'Well, it's funny you mention that. I'm finding it very difficult to eat at the moment...'

'What do you mean, you're finding it hard to eat? Maurice... he's finding it hard to eat.'

Brian could hear his father in the background stumbling around.

'What do you mean, he can't eat?'

'Your father says, "What d'you mean you can't eat?"'

'Well, every time I try to eat, the phone rings and it's you and dad...'

'That's nice... so that's how he treats us for caring. We're your parents, Brian. Of course, we're concerned about you. It's only natural... Anyway, your dad wants to have a word...'

'Alright, mum...'

'Oh, and I hope your first day of work goes well... Maybe you'll meet a nice Jewish girl there...'

'Hello, son.'

'Hi, dad..'

'Tell me, are there radiators in your flat?'

'Yes, there is a radiator in the room, dad.'

'Does it need bleeding, Brian?... You can't trust these landlords. If it needs bleeding, you'll freeze to death. I can bring over a radiator key if you don't have one.'

'No, it doesn't need bleeding, dad. It's perfectly fine and hot, really hot... Ouch! I just touched it,' added Brian with his hand on the stone-cold radiator.

'Don't do that. You'll burn yourself... Now, I wanted to tell you that I've sent some thermal vests in the post.'

'Thermal vests? Why would I want thermal vests? It's summer.'

'Do you never listen to the long-range forecasts? We're in for a very cold winter. And I don't suppose you have double-glazing.'

'No, I don't have double-glazing.'

'Well, there you are... Susan, he doesn't have double-glazing. What did I tell you?'

And so it went on...

———— ··●·· ————

'Hi, Brian. Very nice to meet you. I've heard great things about you. I'm Bernard, the account director on the Solid Fuel account. Magnus likes to call them 'The Solids'. And this is a really important brief. So no pressure...'

Bernard was a tall and imposing character with a neat goatee beard and a black cashmere polo neck. He was most definitely public school material and gay.

They were in Magnus's office and Penny had just brought in a tray of tea and coffee to accompany the plate of tempting chocolate biscuits from M&S.

'Excuse me for butting in, Bernard. I'd just like to give the boys a bit of background.'

'By all means, Commander...'

'Basically, we're trying to persuade the client to run a classic branding campaign for real fires that isn't built around specific product benefits... They are obsessed with things like reducing condensation and the efficiency of burning solid fuel in stoves. But we've been trying really hard to get them to just focus on the beauty and emotional rewards of an open fire, and they are only now beginning to listen, and have actually agreed that we should work up some concepts for their consideration. I think we should concentrate on an idea that will work for TV and 48 sheet posters.'

Angus helped himself to a couple of biscuits and looked at Magnus. 'What kind of budget do we have?'

'That depends on how much the client likes your idea. If they like it, we'll have enough... If they love it, we'll have more than enough.'

Bernard removed a wad of typed-up creative briefs from his attache case and distributed them. 'As you can see, the brief is really very simple. The proposition is very straightforward: 'Enjoy the beauty and warmth of a real fire.' So we want a neat, simple and appealing campaign that conveys that message loud and clear... Once we have it, we'll run it up the old flagpole and see if our jolly old client salutes it. What do we think?'

Angus put his coffee down. 'I think it's a brilliant brief. It's nice and open-ended and gives us a pretty broad canvas... How long do we have?'

Bernard sucked air between his teeth in much the same way as second-hand car salesmen do. 'Well, I'm afraid, we don't have a huge amount of time. The client has already bought a fair bit of air-time at a discounted rate for October, which sounds like a long way off, but it isn't really when you take into account the umpteen rounds of research we'll need to arrange, and presentations we'll be making to all the affiliated bodies... Then there's production time; post-production - not to mention ASA approval. So we really need to get back to the client as soon as.'

'The boys are going to need a minimum of two weeks. As will I.' Magnus grinned at Angus and Brian. 'You have competition, lads. I'm working on it too... Anyway, what do we think?'

Brian coughed and made his first contribution. 'I agree with Angus. It's a really open brief... Are there any avenues we should avoid?... Any pet hates the client has?'

Bernard laughed. 'Sounds like you've already met them... They are a humourless bunch of automatons - pretty dead from the neck upwards. But we've been educating them and nudging them gently in the right direction. And to be fair, the press work they have recently bought is so much better than the garbage they used to run. So I wouldn't hold back. Let's try and sell the fuckers something we'd all be proud to see gracing our screens. Am I right in saying that, Commander?'

'Absolutely. Thing is, this could so easily be an award-winning piece of business. I mean, real fires are bloody fantastic, aren't they? Everyone loves them. So we're halfway there. All we need is a cracking idea.'

'Couldn't agree more. Any other questions?'

Angus munched on another chocolate biscuit and looked Magnus in the eye. 'Yeah. Who's on for a liquid lunch? And more importantly, does the consensus favour the Thirteen Tampons or The Old Trout?'

The Sun and Thirteen Cantons (affectionately known by the creative department as The Tampons) won hands down. It was, after all, within staggering distance.

CHAPTER FOUR

If he wasn't getting worked up about the family business that ran Cranberry Crunch, the nation's most popular breakfast cereal, or getting hot under the collar over some article he'd just read in the Daily Telegraph, Lord Cecil Allard would be letting off steam to Cynthia.

'Those damn bastards are ruining us, Cynthia.

'I knew I shouldn't have appointed them... Should have known better... Losing my touch... If I'm not careful, they'll piss our entire marketing budget away on some damn TV campaign that wins those arseholes accolades and loses me business. Awards! Who needs 'em? No more than bloody farts in a paper bag if you ask me. Do you hear me, Cynthia?... Bloody farts in a paper bag... You listening to me, Cynthia?'

Cynthia grunted and then farted rather loudly herself.

'Yes. I knew you'd agree with me, old girl.'

The thing about wild boar is that they are incredibly loyal and extremely intelligent creatures. You really do know where you stand with a wild boar. And you could certainly get a great deal more common sense out of your average wild boar than the man on the street. This, at any rate, was the view held by Lord Cecil Allard.

'Alright... alright. It's coming.' He sprinkled feed into the trough as well as scattering some on the ground.

Lord Allard had been the first in the country to start a herd of wild boar and had purchased his stock from some surplus animals in London Zoo. Having successfully reared these prize-winning beasts on the smallholding attached to his estate, he had been supplying the likes of Harrods food hall and other select butchers up and down the country. An eight-month-old boar is half the weight of a pig the same age. And they produce litters less frequently than pigs, and when they do, produce fewer offspring. As a result, wild boar will never be cheap meat.

So, in short, they made bloody good meat, not to mention bloody good listeners.

He closed the gate to the hog pen and worked his way through the walled kitchen garden and the orangery, which led him to the back of the house. It was a sizeable property for a family of four, but now that he was on his tod, it was positively gargantuan. His wife had run off with the plumber three years ago, and their two children had flown the nest with their respective partners but were both an integral part of the family business. Mark Allard, the eldest son, was the company's finance director. He was well qualified having breezed through all the accountancy exams with flying colours. His younger brother Tarquin was a talented artist and had studied portrait painting at the Royal College of Art. On graduating, his father had persuaded him to join the family business as its marketing manager; a position he had never felt particularly well qualified or comfortable with.

Lord Allard plonked his tired frame in his favourite room, the kitchen and warmed himself by the Aga. There on the table before him lay the latest accounts and sales projections from Mark. They were not very encouraging. Having been a market-leading breakfast cereal for more years than Lord Allard could remember, these latest figures for Cranberry Crunch were very worrying indeed.

He took hold of the phone. It may have been a Sunday morning but this was important. He wasn't going to wait until Monday.

'Hello. Is that Helen?... Yes, I do know that it is Sunday... And I am well aware that it is 6.30 in the morning... Well, some of us have had breakfast, read the Telegraph and fed the porkers... I said "porkers" not "walkers". Wouldn't want to feed them... Bloody trespassing on my land... Buggers don't need feeding; they need shooting... No, I didn't phone to tell you that... I wanted a word with your husband... What do you mean he's not available?... He's what?... He's snoring... My God, he sounds just like Cynthia... No, I haven't shacked up with some woman... Who do you take me for?... Cynthia is one of the porkers... I said porkers, woman... Can't you get it into your thick head that I can't abide walkers?... And I most definitely haven't shacked up with one of them... I suggest you give him a sharp prod in the ribs... No, I'm not trying to be rude... Yes, I know you have a PhD.... I am not saying you are stupid - although I know plenty of people with PhDs who are frankly thick as pig shit...'

At this point, the phone went dead. That ghastly woman was impossible. If the truth be known, all bloody women were impossible. There was nothing for it but to revisit Cynthia - she was the only bloody female he could talk to.

'It's all fuzzy. Looks like an impressionist painting of a foggy day.'

Angus stretched across and altered the focusing ring on the eyepiece of the telescope. 'You need to bring it into focus, Magnus.'

'Whoh! Stop right there... Oh, my word. I see what you mean about beautiful plumage...'

'I don't mean to interrupt the flow of creative juices...'

Silas Wilcox was a junior account handler on the Solid Fuel account. He may have been wet behind the ears and totally inept most of the time, but he had an incredibly thick skin and an extraordinary propensity to create the impression that he was in full possession of the facts and was very much in control when, in fact, neither was the case.

'I can always come back if it's a bit of an inconvenience, chaps...'

'No, no... that's alright, Silage. Why don't you take a pew?... And if you're a good fellow, Angus here might let you have a look through his telescope.'

'Wouldn't have thought you'd get much birdlife to spy on round here.'

'You'd be surprised... She really is something.'

'Anything rare?'

'Don't know about rare... Just a pair of great tits... Ah, she's flown the nest... Magnus pulled himself away from the telescope and eyed up Silas in the doorway. 'So what can we do for you, Silage?'

'Bernard just wanted to know if we could have a catch-up meeting this afternoon. He's seeing the client later and thought it might be a good opportunity to give the client a flavour of our thinking.'

'I don't mind having a progress meeting between us. But I'm not keen to give the client a sneak preview. That's a bit of a dangerous game. You see, I think the chaps here have come up with something a bit special. And I think it best if we keep our powder dry... Wouldn't want to give them the willies too early on if you catch my drift.'

'No... One wouldn't want to do that... Shall we aim for 3 o'clock then?'

'What do you reckon, Angus?'

Angus bit his lip. 'That kind of depends on Brian...' They all looked over to the corner of the room where Brian was half immersed in the large hood of a grant projector used to blow up images by projecting them onto a glass screen that could then be traced onto layout paper.

'Yeah... 3 o'clock will be fine. I'm just doing the last layout as we speak.'

'Good man; 3 o'clock it is.'

———— ··●·· ————·

'Hello, dad. Sorry about earlier... Well, you know she's a bit sensitive... I know you weren't trying to insult her... Well, actually I think you'll find that the snoring thing is genetic... Mum always used to say the same about you...

'Yes... I have seen Mark's accounts and projections... Well, I don't think I'd have described them in such graphic and negative terms... I think I might have said "disappointing" or "below par"... No, I'm not trying to make light of them... Do you really think that's necessary?... A complete overhaul of our marketing strategy?... And you want those marketing Johnny arseholes in London to be given short shrift... And you want me to sort it out... Are you sure about this, dad?... No, I am not trying to be obstreperous... But - I mean they've won us all those awards, including that Cannes Gold Lion - the one you use as a door-stop... Alright, there's no need to shout. I can hear you perfectly well.

'No, I can perfectly understand how you are feeling... Leave it with me.'

Tarquin put the phone down and his wife put her arm around his shoulder.

'So the old bastard wants you to fire the agency.'

'Not exactly... Well, indirectly, I suppose, yes... He wants them to re-pitch for the business. It's a nice way of telling them to piss off.'

'Your dad being nice. Now there's a thought,'

'It's about as nice as he ever gets.'

CHAPTER FIVE

———— ·•●•· ————

'Ere ye go, guvnor, Obart Ouse number 40 Grosvenor Place.'

Magnus paid the cockney cabbie a fiver. 'Thanks. Keep the change.'

'Blimey! That's very kind of you. Thank you kindly... '

As Brian, Angus and Magnus tentatively edged forward towards the front doors with its Grecian-style columns, the taxi did an illegal U-turn and its owner waved at them. 'Be lucky!'

Magnus chortled. 'We could do with a bit of that. Come on chaps. We're going over the top.'

———— ·•●•· ————

This place reminded Brian of the Passport office, where he'd worked as a student during the summer holidays. It had that same feel to it. It had all the pretence of a grand building in a premier location, but in reality, it was nothing more than a shabby excuse for a building with a rather depressing air. It was one of those offices, he thought, that was well past its use-by date. One that in years to come, the developers would no doubt pull down and start again.

The meeting was scheduled for 11.00 and they were five minutes early. At precisely 11.00 the door opened and an elderly lady in black and white attire pushed an aluminium tea trolley of similar-looking vintage into the room. It was laden with utilitarian tableware and a selection of unappetising biscuits and slices of garish pink and yellow Battenberg cake.

'Good morning, gentlemen. Can I offer you refreshments?'

'That's very kind. I'd love a coffee.'

As the tea lady served Magnus, the team of marketing men from the Solid Fuel Advisory Service entered the room. The Marketing Director Geoff Vickery, a large man with little in the way of hair and a ruddy complexion, clasped Magnus firmly by the hand. 'Very nice to see you again, Magnus.'

'Likewise, Geoff. Allow me to introduce you to our new creative team. Angus is the copywriter and Brian is the art director.'

'Very nice to meet you, gentlemen... I do hope you have enjoyed working on our business... I'm Geoff and this is Alex and Simon. We are the hub if you like of the marketing team for the Solid Fuel Advisory Service. Once we are happy with your work, it's basically down to us to sell it to our affiliate members.

'Now, Magnus has done a sterling job in getting us to re-evaluate our marketing position and our creative work. And to be honest, it's been a difficult process for all of us. And I'd be the first to admit that as an organisation we had become rather set in our ways.

'But the good news is that things are slowly beginning to change. The new press campaign has been a departure for us, and is, I'm pleased to say, being very well received by both our members and the general public at large. In fact, I'd like to go through some focus group findings with you Magnus, after this meeting.

'Anyway, that's enough from me. We're all very excited to see what you lads have come up with to help put real fires in the public consciousness.'

'Thanks, Geoff. Well, I have to say that I'm really excited too and a touch nervous, because inside this portfolio is a TV and poster campaign that is, in my opinion, some of the best creative work our agency has produced since we opened our doors for business back in 1970. The boys have come up with a cracking idea that will undoubtedly get the nation talking. So without further ado, I'm going to hand you over to Angus and Brian to talk you through it.'

Angus and Brian took to the floor. While Brian removed a stack of boards from the portfolio, Angus gave a little introduction.

'The great thing about working on this piece of business is that you guys are selling a really great product. I mean, nobody really has a bad word to say about real fires. They are universally loved. And let's be honest, there is no competition. A radiator, electric fire and gas fire are no competition. They are all ugly as sin. A real fire is a thing of beauty. Open any one of the countless interior design magazines now being published, which incidentally are increasing their circulation, and you'll be confronted with real fires.

'So what we wanted to focus on was the word 'warmth'. Not just the warmth that a real fire generates physically, but the warmth we all feel emotionally towards it.

'At this point, I'd like to hand over to my able assistant Brian.'

Brian stepped forward with a stack of white boards.

'Okay... So we wanted to convey this warm feeling that real fires engender. And we thought, how do we do that in a really memorable way? We had several ideas, but one really appealed to us. It's a very simple idea that we think has legs. So I will show you our TV campaign first.

'Imagine if you will a very pleasant sitting room and a lovely open fire sizzling in the grate.' Brian revealed his first board depicting a beautifully rendered fireplace with said real fire.

'Now imagine that we are listening to a piece of music; a classic love song like Al Green's 'Let's Stay Together'. The camera pulls back and we get to see two figures from behind sitting in front of the real fire.' Brian revealed his second board showing the silhouette of the couple on the sofa. 'Now the camera moves slowly round and reveals our two people on the sofa to be none other than Brian Clough and Don Revie, those two arch-enemies now arm in arm apparently very happy in each other's company. Brian plants a kiss on Revie's cheek. We fade and the final thing we see on screen is your logo and the line: Everyone warms to a real fire.

'In the same vein, other executions could include Michael Parkinson cosying up to Rod Hull's Emu; Mohammed Ali with Joe Frazier; Harold Wilson with Edward Heath; the big bad wolf with Little Red Riding Hood; and Tom Baker as Dr Who with a Dalek.'

Brian placed the keyframes of the TV commercials and the new strapline and logo on a conveniently placed dado rail that ran across the wall.

'Naturally, any of these commercials would make effective 48-sheet posters.' To the currently displayed boards, he added two poster designs - one depicting Dr Who sharing a mug of coffee with a Dalek and Michael Parkinson cosying up to Emu.

Brian sat down and there followed an extraordinary silence. It was as if all three clients were too afraid to speak.

Geoff was the first to break the silence. 'Thank you, Brian and Angus... I'm staying silent because I'd like to hear the views of my colleagues first. Alex, would you like to share your thoughts with us?'

Alex coughed nervously. 'Well, I think the layouts are very nicely rendered... but I wonder if the concepts are just a bit flippant. Our affiliate members are very serious people and I worry that this approach is just too lighthearted.'

'Thank you, Alex. And Simon, what do you think of this campaign?'

Simon stood up. 'I think that it's a clever idea. But like Alex, I'm a bit worried that it might be too clever. And I do worry that our affiliate members won't really get it.'

Magnus had a distinct feeling of deja vu. *Here we fucking go again*, he thought to himself. But he was going to hold fire until Geoff had had his say. And it was strikingly unusual for Geoff to take such a back seat.

Geoff got to his feet. 'Gentlemen thank you again. Alex and Simon. I hear what you say. But I respectfully disagree with your concerns... We are no longer in the business of producing serious ads that bore the pants off our audience... Frankly, I don't care what our affiliate members think... I am more interested in what the punter on the street thinks... And I reckon these ads will make 'em smile. Yes, they are flippant. Yes, they aren't serious. And gentlemen, I do believe that these ads might very well make us famous.

'Now my only real concerns by the way are about usage rights... I mean, the Dr Who concept, which I have to say is terrific and is my personal favourite... How likely is it that we'll have permission to use it?'

Magnus couldn't believe what he was hearing. Geoff who had usually been such hard work was finally coming around to their way of thinking. 'Thanks, Geoff. We really appreciate that. And I'm really pleased you asked that question. Because as an agency, we never present work that can't be produced. So you'll be interested to know that our production department has already spoken with the actor Tom Baker's agent. Because he is no longer appearing in the BBC production, he is free to appear in commercial work, and the BBC do not possess intellectual property rights over his long woollen scarf and hat that we associate him with in the TV role. More significantly, the BBC doesn't even own the rights to the Dalek character, which is owned by the estate of its creator, Terry Nation. We spoke to Terry's daughter this morning, and she would be more than happy for us to use the Dalek character in a TV commercial, so long as you made a contribution to her favourite charity - Cancer Research. I suggested £1,000 and she seemed very happy with that.

'As for the use of Michael Parkinson, he isn't tied to his BBC contract and is free to do commercial work. We only have to be careful not to have him in his famous interview chair in a studio setting, which of course we wouldn't. Brian Clough and Don Revie are also both up for it. Their fees might be a bit steep but we could probably negotiate them down a bit. The same goes for Frazier and Ali. In principle, they are all up for it.

'This is fantastic, Magnus... I think I'm going to have to present this to our affiliates pretty sharpish... I wonder if there's a clever way to present to this bunch... To be perfectly honest with you Magnus, they are all pretty dead from the neck upwards.'

Magnus laughed. 'I'm sure that's an exaggeration.'

'You haven't met them...'

'Well, look we could probably get Tom Baker to present the idea and build the cost into the production fee while guaranteeing him the role.'

'Now, that Magnus is a bloody stroke of genius... If that doesn't ignite a rocket up their collective arse and get them excited, I don't know what will...

'And as for the Brian Clough and Don Revie concept. Why don't we run that as a Christmas spot, and have them kiss under a sprig of mistletoe?'

'Ooooh - that's a thought. Lads - what do you reckon?'

Brian and Angus nodded in unison. 'I think it's a nice idea. What do you reckon, Brian?'

'Yeah. I like it... We could have a bit of fun with Christmas jumpers and football baubles hanging from a Christmas tree.'

Geoff laughed. 'That would be a nice touch, lads... The more I think about it, the more I'm liking this campaign... I'd like you to put costings together for all your executions except Little Red Riding Hood. I think using real people is much stronger. And please do include costings for the two 48-sheet posters. And don't forget to include the Tom Baker presentation idea.'

Magnus was feeling elated. This meant that there was every chance of getting the concepts through the approval process. From his experience, when clients were able to contribute something to the creative process, no matter how small, they tended to take ownership and fight the good fight. 'That's not a problem, Geoff. We'll get onto that straight away. And if Tom Baker isn't available for the presentation to your members for one reason or another, we could arrange for him to do a recording. But obviously, if he can do it in person, that would be preferable.'

'Yeah. Absolutely... And I'll be able to get his autograph... This is great. Thank you for all your hard work. Do we have any more questions before we get onto other stuff?' He looked at his two sidekicks who shook their heads sheepishly. 'Well, I think we've got ourselves a cracking campaign. Are we happy?' he asked his two colleagues rather pointedly.

They both smiled nervously and feigned excitement.

'Great. In that case, let's move swiftly on to other matters. I only have fifteen minutes...'

CHAPTER SIX

— ·•·· —

'Hello, *Gordon Deedes Rutter* speaking. How can I help you?'

'Hello. Could I speak to John Josling please?'

'Yes, of course. Can I tell him who's calling?'

'Yes... sorry, it's Tarquin Allard here.'

'Thank you, Mr Allard, I'll try the line for you...'

A burst of *Greensleeves* crackled through the receiver for a few seconds and then the young girl's voice returned.

'I'm sorry, Mr Allard but Mr Josling is out of the building at present, would you like to leave a message with one of the account handlers?'

'Oh, right... Yes, I'll leave a message with one of the team. Thank you.'

'OK... I'm putting you through now...'

'Hi there... Silas Wilcox at your service. Can I be of help?'

'Hello, Silas. This is Tarquin Allard, Marketing Manager of Cranberry Crunch.'

'Ah... My favourite cereal... I don't actually work on your business, Mr Allard. I work on the Solid Fuel Advisory Service account. But having said that, I did have a bowl of your cereal this morning...'

'Right... Excellent... Always nice to speak to a loyal customer... Is there any chance I could speak to one of the account handlers - Alan Jenkins or Jessica Conrad perhaps?'

'I'm sorry. I think they are all on a bit of a jolly today... Well, I say jolly, but it's more like a kind of an away-day bonding session - if you know what I mean.'

Christ! Perhaps his father was right about this lot. 'Yes, I do know what you mean.' *Bloody piss-up at our expense; that's what it means.* 'In that case, could I ask you to leave a very important message with John Josling?'

'Certainly.'

'Could you ask him to call me as a matter of urgency? I really need to speak to him as soon as possible. He has my number.'

'No problem. I will leave a note on his desk.'

'Thank you, Silas... And keep eating the Cranberry Crunch.'

———— ··●·· ————

'Tarquin, it's John Josling here.'

'Hi there John. Thanks for calling back. I'm afraid dad's been throwing one of his wobblies. He's not a happy bunny... The latest sales figures aren't good I'm afraid.'

'Is he firing us, Tarquin?'

'Not in so many words... He's going to invite six other agencies including yourselves to re-pitch for the business...'

'That's just a nice way of telling us to piss off.'

'...I wouldn't say that...'

'Really?'

'Look - I just want to say that I don't have any issues with the agency's work. All the tracking studies have been pretty good and brand awareness remains pretty high, as you know, but you know what the old bugger's like. Anyway, he's going to arrange a full day and night's accommodation down at Dingleberry Hall for a full briefing. If nothing else it'll be a bit of a jolly for you boys.'

'Right.' *Dingleberry fucking hall? What kind of name was that*, he wondered?

'If the other agencies come up with garbage, there is still a good chance that you could retain the business. It's not out of the question.' But it was, admittedly, about as likely as circumnavigating the globe in a pedalo.

CHAPTER SEVEN

—— ··●·· ——

There were about sixty affiliated members sitting in the largest meeting room in Hobart House. They all had visitor lanyards around their necks. They were all men. They all wore suits and ties. And they were all anxious to hear what Geoff had in store for them.

Geoff, Alex and Simon approached the room with all the work compiled in folders for all the delegates to take away.

'Right. Now I want to see a bit of positive energy from you two today… And if any of them want to pick holes in this work, I'm expecting you two to fill them sharpish with a fucking barrel-load of top-grade Polyfiller. D'you hear me?'

He pushed open the door.

'Gentlemen. Welcome…' He had about five minutes to give them a bit of preamble before wheeling in his secret weapon. Part of him was a little bit nervous, but another part of him was relishing the opportunity to surprise the fuckers with a bit of theatre - something that might actually get them a bit excited for once.

'Now, I'm sure you are all very eager to know what the Solid Fuel Advisory Service proposes in terms of its marketing for the forthcoming year. I will get onto that shortly. But firstly, I'd just like to say that following the new press advertising campaign, sales of real fires in the UK have seen a modest rise across the country, with the most significant uplifts in the South - in particular, London. Brand awareness has, as you know, also been rising, which bodes well for future sales. Now, we have for a long while been discussing the merits of a brand awareness campaign. And today I am very excited by our agency's creative solution. It is, in short, a memorable TV and poster campaign that will, I believe, make us famous and get people talking. But for now, I am going to shut up... I have said more than enough. I'm going to hand over to Alex here who will give you a little bit of an introduction to the work.'

Alex got to his feet. 'Thank you, Geoff. As you know, we briefed our advertising agency to create a memorable branding campaign based on a very simple proposition: *Enjoy the beauty and warmth of a real fire.* And the agency has, we think, created something really special. And to present this new campaign, we have invited someone very special to be with us today. So without any further ado, I'd like our special guest to take to the floor.'

An old boy with thinning grey hair and a beard arose from his chair with a walking stick and shuffled to the front of the hall with some difficulty. Once in front of his audience who seemed totally nonplussed, he glared at them through his spectacles. He then uttered the following words in a rather reedy South London accent:

'Christ, you look like a boring bunch of individuals... It's not a funeral... Come on, smile... It won't bloody kill you... Tell you what, I'll relieve your utter boredom...'

With that, he removed his spectacles, dropped them to the floor and stamped on them. Then he tugged at his face and removed what looked like slivers of flesh. And finally, he tugged at his beard and hair and totally removed them.

There was an enormous gasp from the audience as they now stared at one of the country's best-known actors Tom Baker. And then that very familiar and wonderfully resonant voice sang out.

'That's better... Hello and welcome... I am the Doctor... And I do hope you appreciate me being here, as I had to come all the way by cab... from Alpha Centauri. The meteorite showers on the intergalactic highways make the North Circular look like a picnic... Anyway, here I am in this magnificent... well, perfectly pleasant... if slightly rough round the edges... venue.

'Now, I am very excited because I have been asked to present to you the creative concept for the first TV commercial planned to run this year for the Solid Fuel Advisory Service. And I'm very excited because it stars none other than my good self. However, before I present this lovely piece of creativity to you, I would like to remind you that this work will, of course, finance my next three years of time travelling adventures. So if you don't approve it, I shall hold every single one of you personally responsible.' He gave a deep guttural laugh and the lights dimmed.

A large image of a real fire sizzling in the grate of a fireplace in an attractive living room was projected onto a large screen.

'This, my friends, is the opening shot of our first commercial. The camera pulls back to reveal the silhouette of two characters sitting on the sofa.

'Then the camera gently pans around our subject to reveal yours truly and...'

The image on the screen faded and was replaced by another image of Dr Who and a Dalek sitting on the sofa enjoying mugs of tea.

At this point, the audience laughed spontaneously.

'And now my friends, we come to the very important branding bit.'

The image faded and was replaced with a black screen on which white type appeared and Tom read the line in his warm and inimitable voice: 'Everyone warms to a real fire.'

The audience seemed to love what it was seeing and broke into rapturous applause.

'Thank you, my friends. But we haven't quite finished.'

The room fell quiet once more as another image filled the screen. This time with another real fire in another sitting room followed by Michael Parkinson hugging Emu. This was followed by the Brian Clough with Don Revie execution, and finally the Mohammed Ali and Joe Frazier treatment.

The lights finally came back on, and the audience this time got to their feet and began clapping with even more enthusiasm in appreciation of this showpiece, and Tom Baker took a very deep bow.

Geoff smiled to himself. *Yes, my son. You've only gone and bloody cracked it.*

——— ··●·· ———

'Hello, Magnus. It's Geoff here.'

    'Hi there, Geoff. How's it going?'

    'Yeah... that's why I'm calling... I had the meeting with the fuckers...'

    'How did it go?'

    'To be honest, not great..'

    'Oh fuck!'

'No, it wasn't great... It was fucking brilliant!'

'You bastard...'

CHAPTER EIGHT

Magnus finished his coffee and took his feet off the desk. As he did so, Brian and Angus arrived at his door.

'Come in lads, and close the door.'

The two parked themselves on the sofa and Magnus went and sat next to them.

'It's a funny old world. I used to think that Geoff Vickery was a boring old fart with no imagination. But it turns out I did him a great injustice… He's only gone and bloody sold your work to the affiliates. Mind you, he was given a fair bit of assistance by Tom Baker… But apparently, Geoff has never seen them so animated and genuinely excited. They absolutely loved it, and the budget has been signed off already. We have a production meeting scheduled for next Monday, so I suggest you spend the rest of today looking at as many showreels as possible. We'll need to get some directors in to talk to as soon as possible and make a final decision about who to use.'

Brian placed his A4 layout pad on the desk. 'We've already done that. We have a shortlist of four. It's a really simple commercial in terms of camera moves. But it's the direction of the actors and the lighting that's critical, so we've been through loads of D&AD Annuals and picked directors whose work features great performances and sensational lighting.'

Magnus had a look at the layout pad: *Len Fulford, Ridley Scott, Hugh Hudson and Sid Roberson*. He couldn't argue with that list. They were among the best directors in the business. And the wonderful thing was that they could probably afford any of them.

'That's fantastic. Do you have their showreels in?'

'Yeah. They are all in our office.'

'Great. I'll get them sent over to Geoff. I suggest we get Cathy in production to set up initial meetings with all of them. Then, assuming they are free to shoot when we want to start production, we'll go with our favourite. Then, of course, we'll get pre-production arranged for everyone including Geoff. How does that sound?'

'Sounds brilliant.'

'You two have had the best possible start. The client is ecstatic and you've got a cracking little campaign to produce.' He reached into his drawer and pulled out two envelopes. 'By way of a thank you for your efforts these are for you. Open them in your office. Carry on like this, and you'll soon be earning more than me.'

———— ··●·· ————

Brian placed the envelope on his desk. 'Shall I open mine first?'

Angus grinned mischievously. 'Go on then.'

Brian ran a scalpel down the envelope and pulled out the letter and quickly scanned it.

Dear Brian,

In recognition of your fantastic work, I'd like to raise your salary to £20,000 with immediate effect. On behalf of Gordon Deedes Rutter, I'd like to thank you for your sterling efforts and look forward to working with you in the coming months.

Onwards and upwards.

Yours sincerely,

Magnus O'Shea

Executive Creative Director

Angus stared at his partner. 'You alright, mate? Look like you've just seen a ghost.'

'Yeah... No... It's just that I'm only 25 and I'm already earning more than my old man.'

'Hi there Cathy, this is Louise Buxton speaking. I'm Ridley Scott's PA. I'm calling to pass on two messages from Ridley. He's in New York casting as we speak and he wants you to know that he loved your scripts, which I faxed to him - but he is stacked out at present. In normal circumstances, he wouldn't have hesitated to shoot these commercials for you, but he's already committed himself to doing a really big job for Apple Mackintosh at the moment, and he's not going to be able to meet your schedule. So he's really, really sorry to let you down. He really hates not doing jobs that he believes in. And he really thought he could make your scripts sing.'

'That's a shame, Louise. We love his work... Will you thank him for his kind message and wish him all the best for his latest project.'

'Thank you, Cathy I will. And thanks again for bearing Ridley in mind... I do hope you can find someone who will do a great job for you.'

'Thank you, Louise. Goodbye.'

———— ··●·· ————

Angus tapped on Magnus's door.

'Enter... It's ok... The test match isn't on... And I'm not having a wank...'

Angus and Brian took up their usual positions on the sofa.

'What can I do you for, gentlemen?'

'Just thought we'd give you an update on the production front.'

'Fire away.'

Brian plonked a D&AD annual on Magnus's coffee table. 'This is yours by the way... Ridley Scott can't do it because he has bigger fish to fry, namely Apple Mackintosh.'

'Shame. Silly sod's probably wasting his time on that niche computer brand. It's run by an oddball who doesn't like wearing shoes and socks. In fact, I have it on good authority that he doesn't even wash... This guy I know used to work at Atari with him in New York. Said he smelt so bad that management had to ask him to work nights when nobody else was there.'

Angus laughed. 'You're kidding... His name is... Jobs, isn't it?'

'That's him... Steve Jobs... Apparently, management was too embarrassed to mention body odour - so just suggested that he might prefer working when all the phones were quiet after work. And apparently, that's what he did.'

'Anyway, Sid Roberson is up for it and will be in on Tuesday, as is Len Fulford who will be over on Thursday. Cathy has worked with Len in a previous life. She says he's lovely and really good. He's really hot on lighting as he used to be a stills photographer. Was up there with the likes of David Bailey.'

'Yes, Len is great. He's also been doing it longer, which may not be a bad thing. Personally, I'd probably go with him because he'll almost certainly just aim to get the best from the performer and the lights. He won't try and add something that isn't in the script. You don't want to overcomplicate the thing. Its beauty is its simplicity and wit. Anyway, see what you think. It's your call.'

There was another tap on the door and John Josling poked his head around the door. He was looking troubled.

'Magnus. Do you have a minute?'

CHAPTER NINE

Kenneth Drayton sat at the head of the boardroom table fiddling with his tie. He'd been at the agency as its managing director for three years now and had enjoyed his stint here for several reasons. He shared a love of cricket and good banter with Magnus, who he rated both as an excellent creative director and all-round good egg. And then there was Joan, the archivist - the lovely Joan of Archives with whom he was having an illicit and incredibly passionate affair. She was, needless to say, bloody lovely and fifteen years his junior.

On his watch, the agency hadn't lost a single client and had won a fair number. That unblemished record, however, now looked like it might change.

'Thank you all for coming. I wanted to get you all together to inform you that I have been informed by John that our Cranberry Crunch client is putting its account under review and will be asking us to re-pitch for the business.'

There was a palpable silence. Kenneth poured himself a glass of water.

'As you know, the account is one of our largest clients with whom we have enjoyed a pretty good relationship, so clearly, this comes as a bit of a blow. Though we have been asked to re-pitch, I think we have to be realistic. Very few incumbents tend to retain clients that ask them to re-pitch. Having said this, as a team I think we can be very proud of the work and service that we've delivered over the past five years. Some of our work has been acknowledged by the industry's most respected awards bodies including a Gold Lion from Cannes last year.

'So the question we've been grappling with over the past 24 hours has been whether we should re-pitch. Many agencies would, I'm sure, walk away and not want to invest time, energy and money on chasing a piece of business that was almost certainly going to disappear out the window. But Magnus and I have both agreed that this isn't a lost cause, and I say that for a number of sound reasons. Firstly, we arguably have a better understanding of the brand than any Johnny come lately. Richard and Elizabeth in planning have conducted the most painstaking and illuminating research studies into the sector, and much of these findings could prove invaluable to the client, but the client won't get to see any of it if they decide to part company with us now. Our media buying department has and will continue to secure incredible deals, which will be difficult to replicate. And there's every chance that the client will be unhappy with presentations from other agencies. So for these reasons, we have decided to take part in a creative re-pitch, but Magnus wants to put a fresh creative team to work on it. This is no reflection of the work produced by our current creative teams led by Justine and Hugh, which has been terrific. Magnus feels we need to hit them with something radically different. And he also wants to give Justine and Hugh and the rest of the team a break from the account... I have told the client that we will be happy to take part in the re-pitch, and I'm waiting to hear back from them about timings and so on... Does anyone want to ask me any questions?'

Peter Simons, one of the many account directors sitting around the table raised his hand immediately.

'Yes, Peter...'

'Thanks, Kenneth... First of all, I'd just like to say that I'm obviously sorry to hear that we're going to have to re-pitch... Should we lose the account, how badly will it affect the agency, and is it likely to put some of our jobs here in jeopardy?'

'It's a fair question and one we've looked at with Paul Cox our finance director. The answer is that we should be fine for eight months, assuming that our income from current clients isn't reduced... After eight months, if we haven't picked up new business, the figures won't be looking as rosy as we'd like and we'll have to tighten our belts, which to be honest, may well necessitate some redundancies. But I can assure you that these will be kept to a minimum.'

Kenneth hated these things. They were always so bad for morale. And there was never a good or easy way to convey this kind of shit. 'Anyone else like to ask anything?'

Samantha, one of the small team of planners, raised her hand. 'Do we know why they want to review the account?'

'It's a good question, Samantha. As far as we know, it's simply a response to a bad set of sales figures and projections. These, of course, are unlikely to be directly related to our marketing activity and are more likely to be the result of many other factors like the economy and a changing customer profile. But I'm afraid it's always the advertising that gets the blame.'

'Anyone else?'

The room fell silent. 'OK... That's all I really wanted to say... I'm sorry that I'm the bringer of unwelcome news on a Monday morning. But on a brighter note, I'd just like to share our latest work for the Solid Fuel Advisory Service. I have only just seen it myself, and I have to say that it's really very good indeed. If there's any justice in this world, the strength of this campaign will have other clients soon knocking on our door...'

The lights faded and the large video monitor sprung to life. First up was the Tom Baker and the Dalek commercial, which was greeted by spontaneous laughter. Then Brian Clough and Don Revie kissing brought further mirth, particularly among the men who liked their football. Finally, the Mohammed Ali and Joe Frazier production caused spontaneous applause. For a few moments, at least, everyone in that room had forgotten about the ominous news about Cranberry Crunch. They had all warmed to a real fire.

CHAPTER TEN

— ••●•• —

Brian wasn't used to drinking. In truth, he couldn't really hold his drink at all. It was funny because none of his family or Jewish friends were drinkers either. Drinking and Jews just weren't synonymous. Eating and Jews... now that was something else. Most Jews he knew could eat for England. Having been invited to a post-production lunch that involved indecent quantities of Châteauneuf-du-Pape 1966, it was now with some difficulty that he staggered back to his flat.

He'd moved from the bedsit in grotty old Leytonstone to a one-bedroom flat in leafy, up-market Hampstead with plenty of radiators and double-glazing. And yes, dad, there was even a radiator key!

He stood at the end of Perrin's Walk where Peter Cook lived with his girlfriend. He'd seen him a couple of times in a similar state and once helped him to his front door. He was in awe of the great man and had asked for his autograph and Cook had happily obliged on the back of a Waitrose car parking ticket. It was only later that he'd noticed on close inspection that it actually read *Pissed Cook*.

He could murder a pork pie. It was alright, he was allowed to eat pig as he wasn't an observant Jew - just a hungry one. He stumbled into the small Asian-run supermarket on Fitzjohn's Avenue and picked up a wild boar pie. Wild boar? That was a first. He also picked up a copy of The Evening Standard.

He wasn't sure quite how long it took him to finally get back to the flat but when he did, he sat in the kitchen and devoured the wild boar pie. It was pretty good - rather rich and venison-like, he thought.

He flicked open the Evening Standard.

Stuff about *Margaret Thatcher... NASA launching a space vehicle... The highest price paid for a living artist - £962,200...* More stuff about *Thatcher.* Then something stares back at him that looks ever so familiar. It's a frame from the commercial of Tom Baker having tea and biscuits with a Dalek in front of a real fire. And the headline shouts: *Heartwarming ads we're all going to warm to.*

The piece occupied a whole double-page spread written by an Alison Peterson. He tried to focus on the text:

If these charmingly witty and very English television commercials don't get us all cosying up in front of beautiful real fires sizzling in the hearth this winter, I don't know what will.

I'm sitting in the rather lovely offices of production company Brookes Fulford in North West London overlooking the Regent's Canal. And I'm in the company of one of the nicest and most talented commercial directors of his generation, Len Fulford...

Lots of stuff about directing Tony Hancock back in the 50s for the Egg Marketing Board... blah, blah, blah. Stuff about his time as a stills photographer photographing the likes of Joanna Lumley... And quite a lot of stuff about working on his latest campaign for the Solid Fuel Advisory

Service. And what a joy it was to direct such larger than life characters like... Tom Baker, Brian Clough and Mohammed Ali.

Oh, blimey and here's the clincher.

'Thank you, Alison. I'm really pleased you like it. I don't think it's possible not to like, is it? To be honest, I think it's almost certainly going to be one of the best campaigns I have produced over the years, and certainly the one that everyone will remember me by. And for that I will always remain eternally grateful to both the agency Gordon Deedes Rutter and its very talented creative team of art director Brian Finkle and copywriter Angus Lovejoy for giving me the opportunity to bring their terrific creative idea to fruition.'

———— ·•●•· ————

'Hello Mum, it's Brian.'

'Hello, Brian. Are you alright? You sound a bit strange...'

'Yeah, I'm fine... I think it's a bit of a bad line... I'm just calling to let you know that I'm in the paper today... The Evening Standard...'

'You haven't got yourself into trouble have you, Brian?... Maurice, Brian's in the papers.'

'What d'you mean, he's in the papers?... He's not in trouble is he?'

Perhaps this had been a bad idea... The wine was clearly clouding his judgement.

'No... mum, I haven't done anything to bring the family name into disrepute; not yet anyway. No... the work I've been doing with Angus has been written about in the Evening Standard. And I thought you'd like to know...'

'Oooh, Mazel tov - that's wonderful Brian. I'll get dad to go and buy a copy... And do you mind if I tell Shirley down the road? She's always talking about her son, the accountant. Now I can tell her about our son, the film director.'

'I'm not a film director, mum. I'm an art director.'

'Film director, art director - she won't know the difference. To be honest, between you, me and the gatepost, I think she's going a bit senile...'

CHAPTER ELEVEN

Magnus removed a couple of cold beers from the icebox and offered them to Angus and Brian who were seated in the seats in front.

Brian raised his hand. 'I'm fine thanks, Magnus. It's a bit early for me.'

Angus, who was already necking one, stretched back and took both cold bottles. 'That's ok. I'll have his… Cheers.'

At that moment, the driver of the minibus braked suddenly at a zebra crossing, causing the bottles in the box to jangle in protest.

Angus thought it pretty weird that the client should invite a whole load of advertising oiks down to his country seat just to brief them. His parents who were probably in a similar league to this Allard character and also had a pile in the country, wouldn't have dreamed for one moment of sharing it with the great unwashed.

'So, tell me, Magnus, have you been to Dingleberry Hall before? And what kind of name is that for fuck's sake?'

Magnus downed the last dregs in his bottle. 'No, as a matter of fact, I haven't. Kenneth has had that pleasure. It's apparently rather grand if a little rough round the edges - old money according to him. Family have been landowners for generations apparently. Oh... and Allard is keen on pigs.'

Angus choked on his beer. 'Pigs?'

'Actually, no. I've got that wrong... It's wild boar. Breeds the buggers and sells them to up-market butchers including Harrods.'

Having been half asleep, Brian's ears suddenly pricked up. 'Did you say wild boar?'

'That's right... wild boar.'

'I devoured a wild boar pie the other day.'

'Oh well, you were most probably consuming one of Allard's fine specimens...'

Angus looked at his partner. 'Didn't have you down as a Horrids food hall kind of guy.'

'I'm not. I picked it up in my local food store... I'd hardly call it up-market.'

'As for the name *Dingleberry*', Magnus added. 'I do believe it is a type of cranberry that goes into Cranberry Crunch.'

'Just as well they don't make condoms then,' added Angus. 'Otherwise, we'd be off to *Rubber Johnny Hall*.'

Brian and Magnus chortled.

'On a more serious note,' added Brian, 'I don't suppose we know who we're up against do we?'

'Not entirely... Though we do know that those tossers down the road from us aren't in the frame. I bumped into Tom, their Creative Director yesterday at the gym. He was quite open about it when I asked. Said they were approached but turned it down on account of already working for one of their major competitors... Wouldn't be surprised if Saatchis was going for it though… They seem to get onto most pitch lists these days and aren't bothered by account conflicts as they have a whole raft of sister companies they can farm work out to.'

'That whole account conflict thing is a load of old bollocks though isn't it?'

'Care to elaborate, Angus?'

'Well, I know a guy who works at CBP and he says that the company gets away with account conflicts by simply setting up another company with a slightly different name, and telling the client that their business will be handled by a sister company. But the truth of the matter is that the sister company is in name only and that it's the same people doing all the work. Apparently, when clients come in they are paranoid about keeping all competitors' work out of sight, otherwise they'd be fired on the spot.'

'Yeah… I can believe that… Anyway, I just think that you two should take this thing in your stride. Kenneth didn't want us to re-pitch. He was prepared to write it off, but I persuaded him to let you two have a crack at the brief… And in light of your work on the Solids, he agreed that it was probably worth a shot. So I don't want you to feel constricted or pressurised in any way. Just have a bit of fun with it… All you have to do is produce something you'd be proud to show your mum… I don't care if the client tells us to piss off…'

Angus nodded. He liked Magnus. He was on their wavelength and was a good judge of work. He had a pretty amazing track record, too. The display cabinet in his office was testament to that. Among his collection of metal and perspex on display were Cannes Lions, D&AD pencils, British TV arrows, as well as Creative Circle and Campaign Press gongs. Like a little boy who collected those Esso football club logos pressed out of foil back in the 70s, Magnus had the whole bloody set.

———— • • ● • • ————

Dingleberry Hall was one heck of a pile. Sitting comfortably in the Cotswold hills just outside Chipping Campden, its impressive Victorian edifice hewn from the local golden limestone, shimmered in the winter sun.

'I say Commander. This is a bit of alright, isn't it? Shame we're only here for one night.' Bernard was looking very dapper in his maroon and amber striped blazer and silk cravat and might have easily just stepped off the stage in a production of *The Importance of Being Earnest*. Cranberry Crunch wasn't one of his accounts, but Magnus had persuaded Kenneth to bring Bernard on board, as there was a strange kind of chemistry between him and the boys that seemed to work. They took the piss out of him admittedly, but Bernard gave as good as he got, and underneath the ribbing, there was clearly genuine affection. All three of them could often be spied down at The Tampons after work sharing banter and making each other laugh. Chemistry of this kind between creatives and account management was a rare thing, and Magnus was canny enough to recognise its significance.

Magnus put his arm round Bernard. 'I say, Bernard. You look quite the part... Play your cards right tonight... and you might get lucky.'

'Oh... pull the other one, Commander. You're as straight as they come. And besides, you're not my sort.'

The two giggled as they made their way up the steps to the front doors and into the magnificent entrance lobby.

Kenneth had been right. Dingleberry Hall was indeed grand. The lobby boasted a tessellated marble floor, Grecian columns, a minstrels' gallery and a string of family portraits looking down at them disapprovingly.

An aged butler with white hair and a less than cheerful countenance greeted them and showed them into a side room where a few other guests had already been deposited. They were standing in small clusters and talking in hushed tones while sipping coffee from the family china. They were obviously their competitors.

Magnus was in two minds about talking to the enemy, but he was intrigued to know who they were up against.

'Good morning... Allow me to introduce myself...'

The nearest cluster turned to face Magnus. The tall and gaunt-looking woman with her hair in a bun looked like a Head Librarian, and her equally officious-looking male colleagues in suits and ties could have passed for accountants.

'I am Magnus O'Shea, creative director of Gordon Deedes Rutter.' He extended his hand and the Chief Librarian shook it limply as did her team of accountants.

'Very nice to meet you Mr O'Shea. I am Loretta Hickory-Smithson and this is Jean-Pierre Barnaby, Rupert Anstruther-Gough-Calthorpe, Ralph Heathcote-Drummond-Willoughby and Douglas Twisleton-Wykeham-Fiennes.'

'Excellent... I'd better not ask you the name of your agency then...We could be here all day...' He laughed. But the joke seemed to go over their heads.

'We are the Taylor Agency.'

'Right... The Taylor Agency... I don't think I'm familiar with your company... Are you based in London?'

'No... We are a local agency. Our offices are in Cheltenham.'

'Ah... Lovely. Very lovely city, Cheltenham.'

'Indeed...'

As the housemaid offered Magnus a cup of coffee, more guests spilled into the room and were followed by Lord Cecil Allard himself who was in green wellies and a Barbour jacket.

'Good morning and thank you all for coming. Do help yourself to tea, coffee and whatnot. We're all set up in the library, so when you've finished here, just make your way over - it's down the corridor, beyond the bust of Cicero and it's the second door on the left. We'll start at ten o'clock sharp to go through our new design guidelines and branding initiative. Then we're going to look at competitive branding and positioning. This should take us up to one o'clock when we'll break for lunch in the dining room, and reconvene in the library for the creative briefing at two o'clock. Supper will be served in the dining room at 7.00 sharp. Nothing fancy, just good hearty meat, none of your veggie crap here. And the bedrooms on the first floor all have post-it notes on their doors with your respective names displayed.

'Good... Oh, and there are two bathrooms with WC on the ground floor. I'd appreciate it if the gents could take care not to pee on the floor, as our cleaner is off sick. I will see you in the library in fifteen minutes precisely. Please don't be late as we have quite a lot to get through. And please do not bring your coffee into the library. Thank you so much.'

With that, Allard turned his back on his guests and made his way to the library. He was half thinking of removing his wellies but he couldn't be bothered to go upstairs, and besides, there was every chance that he'd want to have a chat with Cynthia later.

———— ··●·· ————

'Christ, is he always like this?' Angus was never backward in coming forward when spotting an attractive young member of the opposite sex.

The young lady in question had just served him coffee. She was petite, dark-haired, with green eyes and a distinctly coquettish air about her.

'You should see him on his bad days...'

'Wouldn't want to do that... How do the staff put up with him?'

'I wouldn't know... I'm just doing this through an agency... I'm an art student.'

'Oh right. That's great... I love art.'

'Do you paint?'

'I dabble... I could, of course, invite you upstairs to look at my etchings...'

She smiled mischievously. 'And as James Thurber once said, "I could just wait here while you brought the etchings down."'

He laughed. He wasn't expecting that. She was a bit special.

'I'm Angus Lovejoy, by the way.'

'It's very nice to meet you, Angus Lovejoy. I'm Samantha. Samantha Pilkington. But you can call me Sam.'

'Well it's very nice to make your acquaintance, Sam... you'll have to excuse me. I have an appointment to see Lord Allard... But first I must visit his bathroom to pee on his floor.'

———— ··●·· ————

The library was pretty impressive and had that distinct and slightly musty smell of old books that you'd often get when crossing the threshold of a second-hand bookshop. There must have been thousands stacked on bookshelves from floor to ceiling. And many were leather-bound volumes with delicate gold lettering tooled into their spines. All the great names seemed to be present and correct: Dickens, Austen, Shelley, Steinbeck, Orwell, Joyce, Waugh, Hemingway...

Magnus, Bernard and Brian took their seats near the front and Angus arrived next to them a few minutes later. There were twenty seats laid out. Probably five agencies in total, Magnus surmised.

Brian turned to Angus. 'I see you've been eyeing up the local talent.'

'Her name's Sam. Bloody gorgeous. Smart, too.'

'So, I take it you have her number.'

'All in good time...'

The excruciating squelching sound of Lord Allard's wellies on the parquet flooring signalled his entrance into the library. He was followed by his two dutiful sons Mark and Tarquin. The two sons sat down in two designated chairs facing the audience while their father took his place at a dais and tapped on the microphone. It was clearly working and began to make ear-piercing squeals. He took hold of the microphone and bent it in the opposite direction and the electrical squealing ceased.

'Jolly good. I think we can dispense with the technology. I'm sure you can all hear me perfectly well.

'I'd like to start today's session with a presentation of our latest marketing as well as our latest sales figures... Lights please...'

The lights duly faded and a large screen displayed a series of familiar-looking posters, press advertisements, TV commercials and Direct Marketing initiatives. These were followed by a series of extremely dull graphs and pie charts accompanied by the interminable and monotone voice of Mark Allard. This went on for what seemed like an eternity.

Eventually, Lord Allard was back at the lectern looking none too pleased.

'So there we have it... Everything seems to be going tits up... The brand clearly needs to be rejuvenated if we are to succeed in addressing these flagging sales. And to this end, we have been working with a new design agency to put us on the right path. So it is with very great pleasure that I now invite Ogden Baggott, creative director and founder of Ogden Baggott Design Consultancy to step forward.'

Ogden Baggott had been recommended by Lord Allard's cousin Lady Avery, and Baggott who was a very eloquent individual with a sharp intellect had very convincingly implied that all Lord Allard's problems had been compounded by a lack of 'inherent and integrated design.' It was something that Ogden Baggott had specialised in providing for his own clients, and had rectified similar issues faced by many blue-chip names like British Home Stores and BP. It had taken the team at Ogden Baggott several months to create new brand guidelines for Cranberry Crunch and had cost Allard an eye-watering sum of money. But Allard was convinced that this was the secret elixir with which all his new marketing activity could be rebuilt.

The thin figure of Ogden Baggott stepped up to the rostrum and placed a pair of spectacles on his nose, and then proceeded to read from a sheaf of notes in a thin, reedy voice.

Magnus was becoming increasingly incensed by the verbiage pouring out of Baggott's mouth. It was pretentious garbage. Pretentious garbage that was going to profoundly affect every piece of communication the brand was going to create. In the old days, designers were just wheeled in to create a logo and a typeface for headlines. This guy was proposing something far greater. He was dictating the look of every piece of communication; what you could and could not show. But he wasn't happy to confine himself to just the look of the work. Oh no, he was also delving into the brand's tone of voice. Words for fuck's sake that we could and couldn't use. This was fucking advertising by numbers.

From now on the brand was to embrace its serious attributes. Humour degraded the brand attributes and had to be avoided at all costs.

As far as Magnus was concerned, this was clearly a recipe for disaster. This guy's knowledge of advertising could be printed on the head of a pin. Some of the UK's most successful advertising campaigns had employed humour. Bloody Heineken had been doing it for years because it worked. What planet was this blithering idiot on?

Angus and Brian had both nodded off. They thought listening to their own agency planner Richard Deacon wittering on was bad enough, but this guy made Richard look positively riveting. This was painful stuff.

When the lights eventually faded back on, gentle applause woke Gordon Deedes Rutter's star creative team from their slumbers.

Magnus leant forward and whispered into Brian's ear. 'That was about as witty and insightful as Mein Kampf.'

Allard was now back at the Dais in his wellies. 'Thank you for that Ogden... That concludes the first half of our presentation. Lunch will now be served in the dining room.'

Bernard looked at Magnus and rolled his eyes to the heavens. 'I could do with some paracetamol after that... Look, Commander. I think we four should split up and mingle and size up the opposition. What do you reckon?'

'Yes... Good thinking, Bernard... Not sure that we'll benefit in any way, but I'm as intrigued as you are about this lot. I don't see any familiar faces.'

———— ••●•• ————

'I say. I do like your tie.'

Bernard had taken his seat next to the most flamboyant looking guest he could find in the dining room.'

The young man looked at him and blushed. 'Oh, thank you... I wasn't sure if it was a bit louche.'

'Oh no... I wouldn't describe it as louche. No, actually I'm a big fan of Edvard Munch and *The Scream* is such an iconic work, don't you think? But I haven't seen it on a tie before.' It was, he thought, pretty hideous, but also rather appropriate, having sat through that interminable monologue from Baggott.

The young man smiled. 'It doesn't compete with your blazer though. That really is something. Where did you get it?'

'Ah, well that's a bit of a long story. You see it's a family heirloom... Belonged to an uncle who used to play for a cricket club down in Yeovil in Somerset. They were called the Codrington Cobblers. When he died, I went down to his cottage and helped the family clear his house, and his sister said that I could take anything I liked as a memento to remember him by... So I couldn't very well leave his blazer there could I?'

'That's a nice story... Looks as good as new.'

'I don't think he wore it very often... By the way, I'm Bernard Hamilton and I bat for the incumbent, so to speak.'

'Nice to meet you, Bernard. I'm Daniel Day and you probably haven't heard of us lot... I've only just joined as a junior account handler. We are called Aardvarks.'

'Aardvarks? Sounds like another cricket club.'

'Yeah... it does, doesn't it?... Actually, the reason the management chose that name was purely down to the fact that it would appear at the top of the page in Yellow Pages. There aren't many words in the English language that start with a double-A.'

'Right... So what accounts do you work on?'

'To be honest, we don't have any accounts.'

Bernard's jaw dropped in incredulity.

'I know... It sounds crazy, doesn't it? There are only six of us including the two founders John and Phil. Phil is this amazing photographer and his partner was a successful copywriter at RHB.'

'That's interesting... I know a couple of people who are at RHB. In fact, I see a fair bit of them... Can't see them ever leaving the place though... It's all too cosy for them...'

'What do they do?'

'Drink... Yeah, they drink most of the time. Cheap Frascati mainly, and cans of Special Brew.'

'Ok, so they are creatives, right?'

'To be honest, I don't think they are at all creative... No, they're tramps who sit in their doorway.'

Daniel laughed. 'You had me there... That's really funny.'

'So where are you guys based?'

'That's a bit of a sore point at the moment... We have temporary space in Phil's house off the King's Road. His entire basement is his photographic studio. And we have offices in the converted attic... It's far from ideal because he has three really young kids and his thriving studio to oversee.'

'Blimey O'Reilly... That sounds insane.'

'It is to be fair... and I don't think I'm going to stick around more than a couple of months... If they haven't picked up some business and moved offices by then, I will jack it in. It's impossible to work in that kind of environment.'

If they don't pick up business in a couple of months, you might not have a job to leave old boy, thought Bernard. 'So how did you get on Lord Allard's pitch list?'

'That was entirely through Phil... Lord Allard is one of his photographic clients. He shoots his pigs, or wild boar... with a camera, that is, not a gun... He's done a few shoots for Lord Allard's brochures... Bloody smelly and noisy, I can tell you with all those lights and animals down in the basement... Anyway, Lord Allard was over the moon with the results... Thinks Phil is "a bloody genius."'

'Does he now?... How very interesting.'

———— ··●·· ————

Brian stabbed a piece of pink meat with his fork and sampled it. To his delight, it tasted just like the wild boar pie. It had that same distinct venison-like flavour and texture - not that he was some kind of gourmet. But he did possess a fairly good sense of taste.

'Good isn't it? That will be one of Lord Allard's own wild boar you know?' The man sitting to his right was middle-aged and balding, and was, Brian thought, very home counties and decidedly posh. 'The name's Digby, Hugh Digby - Diggers to my friends. And to whom do I owe the pleasure?'

'Oh, I'm Brian Finkle. People just call me Brian...'

'Well, Brian. What do you make of the wild boar?'

'It's pretty good, isn't it?'

'It's the best... Allard is a smart cookie, mark my words... First man to breed wild boar in the UK... and the first to get Harrods to stock it on their shelves... To be perfectly frank with you, the wild boar stands to do an awful lot better than that Cranberry Crunch muck.'

'Is that right?... So, which agency are you from then, Hugh?'

'Oh, I'm not actually from any agency... I'm a farmer... Well, I say farmer. I own a farm... I don't do any of the heavy lifting... Come to think of it, I don't do any kind of lifting. No, I pay for that kind of thing. Having said that, my wife does a fair bit. Don't pay her, of course. She likes doing it. Likes to get her hands dirty, so she says... Bloody good at it though. It's in her family, you know?'

'What's that?'

'Big bones... they've all got 'em. Her mother was endowed with big bones. Runs in the family. Magnificent figure of a woman. Blood fine filly... Anyway, I digress... What's your line of business, Fickle?'

'I'm an art director.'

'Art director, eh? Sounds jolly technical... So you are some kind of architect then, are you?'

'Oh no... I work as a creative person in advertising. So I am tasked with coming up with ideas for ads and then designing them.'

'That's very interesting... I do like a good TV commercial... Some of them are better than the programmes, you know?... There was a terribly good one on the television the other day. What was it for? Ah yes... it's coming back to me... Dr Who on a sofa with tea and biscuits and getting very cosy with a Dalek in front of a real fire... It made us laugh... I don't know how they come up with them. Have you produced anything I might have seen?'

'Er... no, I don't think so... I haven't been doing it long.'

'Ah, shame. Well, I look forward to seeing some of your creations gracing the old telly box.'

'So you're not involved in pitching for the Cranberry Crunch business?'

'Me? Oh, heavens, no... I'm just here to make up the numbers... And lend moral support... That kind of thing... Always happy to accept a free lunch... particularly if wild boar's on the menu...'

'So you're a good friend of Lord Allard, are you?'

'Could say that... I'm family... Well, was family until he divorced my sister... Silly girl... Shacked up with the plumber. Rum fellow if you ask me. Never did fix the cistern in the upstairs bedroom...'

'But you remain good friends.'

'Oh yes... He's a good egg... can be a bit grumpy and curmudgeonly at times, admittedly, but a good egg all the same...'

Sod's Law wasn't it that he'd only gone and sat next to the only person in the room who wasn't involved in the pitch.

The attractive young girl that Angus had been chatting up, collected Brian's empty plate and gave him a knowing smile. He smiled back.

— ·•●•· —

Magnus had avoided the Chief Librarian woman and her team of accountants and had planted himself between a small, rotund and highly animated man in a tweed jacket with leather elbow pads and a surly-looking young man in a denim shirt who looked vaguely creative.

The animated man to his left immediately introduced himself.

'Hello, hello, hello. We have a stranger in our midst. Allow me to introduce myself... My name is Simon Anstruther and I am the founding partner of Anstruther Powel and Partners. And to your right is David Jansen, our head of strategic planning.'

David nodded and feigned a smile, which was clearly a bit of an effort.

'Hi there. I'm Magnus O'Shea...'

'Of course... creative director of Gordon Deedes Rutter... It's a real pleasure to meet you, Magnus... And let me say here and now that I think your recent campaign for real fires is an absolute bloody masterstroke. It's quite the best thing on the telly at the moment. Many, many congratulations.'

'That's very kind of you. Thank you, Simon… We are quite proud of it…'

'Well, you have every right to be… And I'm not just saying this as friendly chit-chat… Not at all… I seriously think that your campaign is up there with the greats. In years to come it will no doubt pass into advertising lore and be remembered fondly with the likes of the Cadbury's Smash Martians and Heineken's Refreshes the parts campaigns… It will take its place in the Advertising Hall of Fame.'

'Well, we can live and hope… So tell me, Simon, do you do much work for the food and drink sector?'

Simon paused for a moment to check that nobody was within earshot and then lowered his voice to a conspiratorial whisper. 'Well actually, no… and frankly, we can't work out why we have been invited to pitch… I think it's through Ogden Baggott. We did some work with him a couple of years ago, and I think he put in a good word for us. But to be honest, we are not an above-the-line agency like yourselves… Never have been… No, we know our place, as Ronnie Corbett once said…' He laughed and Magnus laughed with him out of embarrassment. 'No, seriously - we are at the grubby end of the spectrum; we are direct marketing specialists - envelope stuffers, for which we get reasonable results - not gold Lions at Cannes. We don't sell ourselves as a creative operation. So we are, as I say, a bit nonplussed by all this. But we're not ones to turn down a challenge.'

Magnus was gobsmacked by Simon's honesty. It was refreshing in an industry that was full of so much bullshit. And in a strange kind of way, he admired Simon for it. But like Simon, he, too, was perplexed by Allard's choice of agencies. Perhaps Kenneth had been right all along for them not to get involved. If it transpired that all Allard was looking for was a bloody direct marketing campaign that adhered to a set of mindless design guidelines, then they'd all be wasting their time.

'Thank you for that, Simon. And I don't blame you for rising to the challenge. After all, it's a nice chunk of business and will always look good on your client list. But if Allard is after a direct marketing campaign, my agency will be wasting its time.'

Simon leaned closer. 'I suggest we wait for the briefing... If you're right, I think he'd be nuts... because he's always going to need a brand-building advertising campaign. But if you're right and he does want to go down the direct marketing road, it might be worth us putting together a joint proposal - if, of course, you were interested... You could lead with an above-the-line creative brand campaign and we'd support it with integrated direct marketing. We could sell it as 'integrated marketing.' You have the creativity and we have the number-crunchers...'

Magnus nodded. It was a pretty good plan. And it wasn't as if the agency weren't averse to shovelling a bit of shit. Danny had been producing tons of steaming horse manure for Marshall Cavendish for years. At least, with this arrangement, it wouldn't be their horse manure. And at least Simon knew it was horse manure. Poor old Danny thought he was cronking out little gems and once famously equated advertising to interior design. Magnus smiled to himself as he remembered one of Kenneth's priceless quips. 'That man isn't an interior decorator', he'd said, 'He's an internal defecator. The man doesn't know shit from sausages.' Magnus chuckled to himself. 'Do you know, Simon, I think you may have hit on something.'

———— ··●·· ————

As luck would have it, Angus found himself between two members of the opposite sex. For once, it wasn't out of choice. It was the only empty seat between two people that he could find. To his left was a frumpy middle-aged, middle-of-the-road, middle-class housewife who looked like she'd rather be at her local townswomen's guild meeting. And to his right was a studious-looking girl in bright red spectacles and slightly militant looking dark green dungarees.

'Hi there. I'm Angus... Sorry, I didn't catch your name...'

The frumpy woman answered without even looking at him.

'That's because I didn't offer one up.'

'Ah, that would explain it... What kind of communications agency do you work for? I wonder. Might it be Boorish Churlish Moody and Partners?'

'I suppose you think you're being funny... Do you know who I am?'

Angus turned to the girl in dungarees. 'Excuse me. The lady sitting next to me doesn't seem to know who she is. Could you help her out?'

The girl put her hand to her mouth in an attempt to stifle her giggles.

'You really are a smart arse, aren't you?'

'To be honest, I'd rather be a smart arse than a dumb arse.'

With that, the frumpy woman rose from her seat. 'I'm not putting up with any more of this bilge.'

'Oh, shame... That was just the warm-up act... No refunds I'm afraid... What's got into her? Ah, maybe that's the problem... Perhaps no one's getting into her...'

The girl in dungarees blushed and waited for the older woman to disappear. 'You could be right... She's always like this. She's a complete nightmare and a total control freak.'

'And don't tell me... Those are her good points.'

The girl laughed again. 'Don't know why I'm laughing... I have to work for the bitch.'

'So is she the top banana?'

'Yeah. Afraid so... I'm Jennifer by the way.'

'Hi, Jennifer... My commiserations... So what's the company?'

'You ready for this?'

'I'll brace myself shall I?'

'We're called Creative Genius, and that charmer of a woman is Alex Hillingdon. It's her company. We're a small agency in Brighton and I'm the creative department.'

'Oh wow... So you're the genius behind the name then.'

'Hardly... She'd never recognise anything vaguely creative if it jumped up her arse and went "whoopee!"'

'Look, I'm not being rude or anything but how did Little Miss Grumpy get on Mr Unhappy's pitch list?'

'One word: nepotism; she's his cousin.'

'Right...'

'It's a strange one though because they aren't especially close as far as I can tell.'

'They both share the same grumpy gene by the looks of things...'

'They certainly do...'

'So are you looking forward to working on this one?'

'It'll make a nice change from Scrivens hearing aids and Sanicare incontinence pads.'

'Oh, I don't know... I wouldn't knock nappies for grown-ups - there's a rich vein of humour to be mined there. Get them to piss themselves laughing, and you'll be selling more product.'

This time she laughed so much that she had to bury her face in a table napkin.

As she did so, Sam picked up Angus's empty plate from behind his shoulder and discretely left a small tab of paper on his table. 'See you later if you're free.' He looked at her impishly perfect features and smiled. Then she was gone.

He discreetly removed the piece of paper, placed it in the palm of his hand and turned it over.

As a piece of copy, it was concise bordering on curt: *Etchings: Second floor. Last room on left (spot of red nail varnish on doorknob) - 8.00 pm?*

CHAPTER TWELVE

— • ● • —

Lord Allard took a sip of water. 'I do hope that lunch was agreeable. As some of you may be aware, the meat provided was our own specially raised prize-winning wild boar, which I'm very proud to say is now being sold in the Harrods Food Hall. Anyway, I digress... To get to the crux of today's gathering, I am going to leave you in the very capable hands of my son Tarquin. And now you will have to excuse me... I have other fish to fry...' And with these words, he made his way out of the library in his squelching green wellies.

Tarquin rose from his chair and placed his script on the lectern, all fifteen pages of it, along with a whole stack of transparencies for the overhead projector. His father had compiled the entire thing with Ogden Baggott. But judging by the jargon and so-called 'buzz words', it had chiefly been the work of Baggott. There were lots of references back to the extensive design guidelines that Baggott had created and countless examples of things the new campaign had to avoid at all costs. And the creative brief clearly specified that above-the-line brand advertising would from now on only be one small weapon in the marketing armoury. Direct Marketing and Direct Response advertising were to feature large with special attention given over to tactical price promotion work, sponsorship and PR. There were in total eight creative briefs written for each discipline, targeting both the consumer and the trade.

Magnus wasn't in the least bit surprised and had warned Kenneth in advance that this might well have been the outcome. As a creative agency, Gordon Deedes Rutter was known for its press and TV brand work that was dubbed by the industry as being 'above-the-line'. Direct Marketing, on the other hand, which was known as being 'below-the-line', was the poor relative and was generally speaking not very creative; displayed large telephone numbers and interest rates; and took the form of small space press ads and mailers. Magnus didn't use the phrase 'below-the-line'. He just called it 'beyond-the-pale.' This said, the agency had at times hired freelancers to produce 'below-the-line' work for pitches and existing clients who very occasionally required it. Kenneth was keen for the agency to take on a full-time 'beyond-the-pale' team, but Magnus had resisted. Of course, Danny, bless him, had produced both 'above' and 'below-the-line' work. But in his case, of course, everything he touched turned to shit.

By tea time, Tarquin had finished the presentation and the lights had come back on.

'That concludes our creative briefing. I hope you found it both insightful and inspiring.'

Magnus chuckled to himself. It was about as inspiring as Carl Andre's pile of bricks in the Tate. Actually, on second thought, that was probably being a bit unfair to Carl Andre.

'Would anyone like to ask any questions?'

Seeing that most in the audience had nodded off during the presentation in the dark, there was a distinct lack of raised hands.

Magnus felt compelled to say something.

'Firstly, thank you Tarquin for a very comprehensive presentation. In light of Mr Baggott's excellent work, and in keeping with this imperative need for integration and synergy across all the brand's communications, would you agree that brand advertising must come before all else and must be developed first? After all, it's difficult to see how one's brand advertising can support the idea behind a Direct Marketing campaign because as we all know, Direct Marketing campaigns aren't usually based on anything remotely resembling an idea.'

Tarquin agreed with Magnus, of course. And had disagreed with his father over appointing Baggott in the first place. As far as he was concerned, this whole thing over design integration and Direct Marketing was a hugely expensive distraction. It wasn't going to solve their problems. But his father was convinced otherwise and wasn't going to back down.

'I hear what you're saying Magnus. But if we all stick rigidly to Ogden Baggott's design guidelines I think all the work will look like it's coming from the same stable, so to speak. So the question of following the style and theme of the brand advertising won't even arise. We will all be singing from the same hymn sheet.'

Magnus smiled and nodded magnanimously. As he had concluded earlier, Baggott had devised a simple formula that clients could buy into while lining his own pockets rather handsomely - it was advertising by fucking numbers. Or put another way, a case of the bland leading the bland.

'Excellent...' Tarquin straightened his tie. 'Well if there are no further questions, I suggest we close today's presentation. We have copies of the brief printed and bound on the table by the door. Please do take copies on your way out. We will, of course, be in touch with all of you in due course to schedule your presentations. We hope to make a decision approximately six weeks from now...

'Supper will be served at 6.30 in the dining room. Until then, you are free to enjoy the house and the extensive grounds. If you are interested in viewing Lord Allard's wild boar, this can be arranged. Just ask any member of staff and they'll direct you to the pen. Oh... and there is a billiards room on the second floor...

'And finally, on behalf of Cranberry Crunch, many thanks to all of you for coming down to Dingleberry Hall today and agreeing to tackle our marketing brief. We really do appreciate it. Needless to say, we really look forward to seeing the results of your endeavours over the coming weeks. Thank you.'

There was a spontaneous round of applause, and the throng slowly made its way out of the library and dispersed.

CHAPTER THIRTEEN

Magnus accepted the cigarette from Bernard on the gravel driveway. 'I shouldn't. I've officially given up, you know.'

'I did wonder... Was it the GP's doing?'

'No... It was Rebecca... She threatened to divorce me if I didn't... She can't bear the stale aroma... And to be fair, it does reek something awful. You only really notice it when you give it up... Still, the odd one won't hurt.'

'As the Bishop said to the actress.'

Magnus chuckled. 'You know Bernard, you are a funny old cove. I suspect that you're a frustrated creative.'

Bernard took a long drag on his cigarette. 'You could be right, Commander... Always wanted to go to drama school when I was younger, but the old folks weren't having it... The old man made me read Law at Trinity... Most boring three years of my life...'

'I don't know about you, but I reckon the last three hours have been the most boring three hours of my life...'

'Do you think we should pull out?'

'It's a pig of a brief.'

'Bloody wild boar, if you ask me...'

'Very good, Bernard... Do you think we should though?... Pull out, that is.'

'Wouldn't be too hasty... I'd ask the boys if they can work with it... Bugger though the brief is, they may still be able to pull something out of the hat...'

'You're probably right... Some of my best work was on crap briefs... Bizarre, isn't it?'

'Snatching victory from the jaws of defeat, and all that...'

'Who did you sit next to during lunch by the way?'

'Nice young lad named Daniel Day. Works for a start-up called Aardvarks founded by a photographer and a copywriter. But get this, their client list is a blank piece of paper.'

'What? No clients?'

'Not a sausage.'

'How the fuck did they get on the pitch list for one of the UK's largest breakfast cereals?'

'Phil the photographer who is the joint founder apparently photographs Lord Allard's wild boar for his brochures, and Allard thinks he's something of a genius with the camera.'

Magnus finished his cigarette and stubbed it out on the gravel. As he did so, they were joined by Angus and Brian.

'Don't suppose I can cadge a fag, can I Bernard?'

'Be my guest.' Bernard offered Angus a light.

'Ta... I've actually given them up - well, sort of...'

Magnus laughed. 'Join the gang... Did you speak to anyone during lunch?'

'Yeah. A complete cow... Think I offended her... Turns out she's Allard's cousin. Her name is Alex Hillingdon and the agency she owns is tiny, based in Brighton, and calls itself Creative Genius... Yeah, I know, subtle isn't it? Accounts include the exotic Sanicare incontinence pads business.'

Bernard laughed. 'Oh, I say. Most de rigueur... So do we think Allard is going to give the business to the Creative Genie Arse?'

Angus blew a perfect smoke ring. 'Well, that's the strange thing, because the other person I was sitting next to was her entire creative department. She clearly isn't a big fan, and seems to think that the cow and her cousin don't get on particularly well.'

Magnus was impressed 'You've done jolly well to extract so much info... How about you Brian. Did you manage to glean anything during lunch?'

'Yes. But not of any great use, I'm afraid. My bloke is called Hugh Digby... Pretty eccentric... Pretty rich I imagine... And only here to lend moral support, so he says. His sister is Allard's wife who ran off with the plumber three years ago. Allard must quite like the guy to stay in touch... Oh, and he loves the commercials for the Solids. It was totally unprompted. He just came out with it...'

Magnus nodded. 'Oh well, he's gone up in my estimation already... All rather baffling nonetheless. I sat next to a Simon Anstruther. Actually, quite a likeable chap who was refreshingly honest. Runs a Direct Marketing company and was a bit taken aback that they were invited to pitch. Reckons it was Ogden Baggott who put in a good word for them. Interestingly, he suggested we join forces and put together a joint proposal... I didn't think it was a bad idea. But I'll have to put it to Kenneth.' He paused and looked at Angus and Brian. 'Bernard thinks I should ask you chaps whether you think we should go for it or not... I'm not putting you on the spot... But once you're back at the office, knock it around for a couple of days... See how you get on... If you think the brief is too much of a straightjacket, we can always pull out, otherwise we'll just go for it.'

Brian nodded. 'Sounds like a good plan.' Angus agreed.

'I just don't get why Allard has approached, what appears to be, a bunch of second-rate amateurs... Bernard, do you recognise anyone from the industry here?'

'Afraid not, Commander... I agree... It's all a bit bloody strange...' His train of thought was broken by the sound of a gong being struck rather rigorously. 'I think that's someone telling us that it's time for supper.'

CHAPTER FOURTEEN

'I say. Would you mind terribly if I joined your table?'

Brian smiled politely. 'Not at all, that's fine... Let me introduce you... This is my partner in crime, Angus Lovejoy.'

Hugh extended his right hand. 'Very nice to make your acquaintance, Angus... I'm Hugh Digby - Diggers to my friends.'

'Nice to meet you, Diggers. I'm known as Aggers to my friends, and Shaggers by this lot.'

Hugh forced a smile, and Brian gestured towards Bernard and Magnus. 'And this is Bernard Hamilton and Magnus O'Shea, our creative director.' Bernard and Magnus both shook Hugh's hand.

'I understand that you are Lord Allard's ex-brother-in-law...' Magnus hesitated for a moment. 'Actually, is there such a thing as an ex-brother-in-law?'

'Good question... If it isn't, it bloody well ought to be... But yes... my sister was married to Lord Allard - until she employed a plumber to sort out the plumbing - course he never did sort out the cistern.'

'Plumbers are the worst aren't they?' said Angus. 'They are as rare as hen's teeth; never show up when you need them; and when they do, they can't wait to get their filthy hands on the old boiler.'

Magnus laughed out of embarrassment. But fortunately, the joke was lost on Hugh who continued the conversation oblivious to the slight to his sister.

'Do you know... I had no idea that advertising was so complicated... That Baggott fellow seemed to have an awful lot to say on the subject. I never knew so much went into a 30 second TV commercial...'

'In truth,' added Bernard, 'we are a bunch of pretentious showmen who like to blind clients with pseudoscience. The truth of the matter is that it isn't complicated at all... The only people who really count are these reprobates.' Bernard pointed at the others. 'You see, Hugh, these clever buggers produce the bloody creative work.'

'I wouldn't put yourself down so swiftly, Bernard,' added Angus. 'This man is a consummate salesman. Given half a chance, he'd sell Hawaiian shirts to the Eskimos and funeral plans to Hindus on the banks of the Ganges.'

Hugh looked a bit nonplussed. 'So how do you go about foisting this Cranberry muck stuff on the general public?'

'That,' chipped in Magnus, 'is the one million dollar question... Particularly when we have to abide by the design guidelines outlined by our Mr Baggott.'

Hugh looked even more confused. 'Well, don't look at me, chaps. I wouldn't have the foggiest where to start.'

'So, I take it, you don't care for the Cranberry Crunch muck,' said Magnus.

'Can't stand the stuff. Too much bloody sugar... I've told Cecil countless times to change the formula. It stands to reason that a so-called 'healthy breakfast cereal' shouldn't carry sackfuls of extra refined sugar. Any blithering idiot can see that. But will he listen?... Only one he listens to around here is Cynthia.'

'That's his girlfriend is it?' ventured Brian.

'Not exactly. It's his prize wild boar. The only one he refuses to send off to the slaughterhouse... Says she's got more bloody sense than his entire family put together.'

'I wonder if Cynthia fancies taking on our creative brief,' wondered Bernard.

'She's bound to trot out loads of layouts, but will probably make a right pig's ear of the copy,' suggested Angus.

'Could save our bacon, though,' added Brian.

'Health and safety won't be happy though,' countered Bernard. 'We'll be breaking all the employment laws. They'll tell us that the arrangement isn't entirely kosher.'

'And they might report us to the pigs,' said Angus.

'For heaven's sake Angus. Stop it, man,' demanded Magnus. 'You're hogging all the bloody puns!... Excuse us, Hugh... Just a bit of childish banter.'

'Indeed...' Hugh seemed oblivious to the gags. 'It hadn't occurred to me that wild boar wasn't kosher... I suppose it makes sense... I imagine they aren't far removed from your common or garden pig.'

'I think you'll find that any animals that are not cloven-footed and don't eat grass are deemed to be unkosher by the Jewish religion,' explained Brian.

'How interesting... I was once taken for lunch to a famous kosher restaurant in London. I think it was in Whitechapel if memory serves...

Very interesting place I have to say... Hive of activity... Very peculiar service, too. Ah yes, now what was it called?...'

'I think you may be thinking of Blooms,' suggested Brian.

'Ah, yes. That's it... Blooms... The food was interesting, but the waiters were even more interesting... I remember being served by a Chinese waiter and one of the diners congratulating this Chinese waiter on his extraordinary ability to speak fluent Yiddish. Seconds later the manager came over and asked him in no uncertain terms to keep quiet about the Yiddish. Apparently, the Chinese waiter thought he was learning English.'

Bernard, who was sipping a glass of water, suddenly choked on it. 'That's very funny...'

'It's famous for its rude waiters,' explained Brian, while patting Bernard on the back. 'People go there, not for the food so much, but for the very creative ways in which its waiters manage to insult the customers.'

'It sounds wonderful,' said Magnus. 'We should all go there for our Christmas creative lunch. What do you reckon?'

All three nodded gleefully. 'Fantastic idea, Commander. And there's a lovely inverted logic to going there for Christmas. After all, Jesus was a nice Jewish boy, wasn't he?'

Angus couldn't resist telling his Jesus Christ joke. '... Alright then, what did the bus conductor say to Christ when he tried to board his bus?' The three others looked at Angus expectantly. 'Look mate, I don't care who your father is, you're not bringing that bloody cross on my bus.'

Hugh particularly enjoyed that one. 'That's very good.'

'Tell you what, Hugh. Seeing that you started this thing, why don't you join us at Blooms.'

'I'd be honoured.'

'Excellent. Bernard, remind me to get onto Penny to book a table when we get back to the ranch.'

CHAPTER FIFTEEN

Angus hadn't played billiards since he was a kid. They used to have a full-size table up in his parents' loft room not dissimilar to this one, and he had tried to misspend his youth in that room honing the few skills he had. It had been a lot of fun playing again. He had beaten Brian and Magnus very easily. Bernard, however, turned out to be something of a demon on the table, having never played before, and the game was a nailbiter, which Bernard eventually won by just three points.

'Fantastic game, Bernard. Well played, mate... You are a bloody natural.'

'Thank you, Angus... I really enjoyed that. I shall have to take this up.'

The two shook hands. And that's when Angus suddenly remembered.

'Oh shit! I almost forgot.' He looked at his watch. It was five past eight. 'Sorry chaps - I'm going to have to love you and leave you - I'm running late for a date.'

'My word... You don't miss a trick do you old boy?'

'Not if I can help it.' And with that, he was off.

The corridor snaked around the house and eventually came to an end by a sash window that looked out onto the garden. He tapped on the door with the red nail varnish on the doorknob.

'You may enter.'

He opened the door and slipped in. The curtains were drawn and the room was reasonably dark.

'You are late... Creative people often are, you know.'

'Yes... I usually am late as it happens... It's a bit dark to inspect your etchings in here.'

She giggled. 'Well, don't just stand there. Get into bed.'

He needed little encouragement.

<hr />

'Hi, sweetie. Just thought I'd call you before turning in.

'Yes, it's been alright... The presentations were pretty turgid to be honest...

'Yes, Kenneth was right. It is quite a place here. You'd love it.

'No... Most people seemed to retire to their rooms after supper. And we just played billiards.

'Any gossip? Well, actually, yes... Get this, Angus has already hit it off with a girl... Pretty little thing.

'No, she's not from one of the agencies. She's the waitress...

'No, I'm not kidding.

'Yes... we did manage to speak to some of our competitors. Strange bunch from the grubby world of Direct Marketing. And one eccentric old boy - Allard's ex-brother-in-law.

'Love you, too. Kiss the kids for me.

'Night night.'

Magnus put the receiver down. He'd been married to Rebecca for eight years and they were still best friends. And there wasn't a minute that passed at work when he didn't feel guilty for being away from her and the kids.

The room had that faded grandeur that came with old money. Everything was old down to the wallpaper and paintwork; even the mounts framing the large hanging watercolours had yellowed with age. The place had history and atmosphere. It had a soul. And no money in the world could buy that.

Magnus climbed into the large bed, turned off the table lamp, sank into the cool linen sheets, and closed his eyes.

———— ··●·· ————

Brian could hardly believe he was living this life. It was only a few months ago that he was living in a squalid bedsit in Leytonstone. Now he owned his own one-bedroom flat in Hampstead thanks to his insane salary and a mortgage from the Nationwide Building Society. He was working for one of London's most creative advertising agencies; having conversations with famous film directors and actors; and dining out at fancy restaurants in Soho. And the strangest thing was that this whole thing didn't feel like work in the conventional sense. It was enjoyable and exciting to create something from scratch and see it come to fruition.

Angus was fantastic to work with. He was funny but also really clever and sharp. Together, they were a perfect creative team, since neither of them was possessive over ideas. They were both just happy to bounce ideas off each other until they had something they both liked. As a result, they had become very good friends.

The only thing Brian was missing in his life was a girl. But in the fullness of time, maybe that too would change.

He brushed his teeth, climbed into bed and switched on his transistor radio:

'We have a Cederic Steebling from Cricklewood. Hello, Cederic.'

'Hello, Clive.'

'Tell me Cederic, what is your take on the miner's dispute?'

'Well. I would say more give than take I think to be honest. Definitely more give than take. I wouldn't want to take anything more away from the miners - no. I mean, mining is a filthy job. Extracting lumps of coal out of the ground is a particularly filthy vocation. And I feel that the filthy nature of the work is something that is so very often overlooked, Clive.'

'Yes. Well, it's a point that not many callers have made. So I take it you have sympathy for the mining communities then?'

'Yes. I have very deep sympathy for the miners. Very deep sympathy. I know you see what it's like digging into the ground...'

'So you do a lot of digging do you, Cederic?'

'Not always personally you understand. But I am very familiar with the rigours of digging. And I must say that digging is a most rigorous activity. Very rigorous indeed.'

'I'm sure it is.'

'One cannot overstate the filthy nature of digging alongside the rigours involved.'

'No. I'm sure that's right. And may I ask why it is that you are so familiar with the filth and rigours of digging?'

'I'm a funeral director...'

'Ah... I wasn't expecting that.'

'That's what my last client said before we buried him...

'Now here's a funny thing. Not that there are many funny things about funeral directing. Funeral directing isn't known for its humour, Clive. But you know we have never gone on a strike - ever. Not even a go-slow.

'Now I know what you're going to say... You are going to tell me that we don't dig as deep as the miners. And you'd be right, of course. We only dig to about two metres. And the average coal mine is about 1,500 metres deep.

'So there are far more rigours involved in the mining. And far more filth. Those levels of rigour and filth would make our job nigh impossible, of course. We have to look spic and span for the grieving relatives. So there is no place for filthy coal dust in the funeral trade. No place at all. Which is why I do have very great sympathy for the miners. Very great sympathy indeed. Of course, as a funeral director, I am no stranger to sympathy and coming over all sympathetic. It is an occupational hazard.'

'Well thank you very much indeed Cederic from Cricklewood for that interesting and memorable contribution tonight. I don't think we'll forget that one in a long while.'

The nasal voice of Cederic sounded vaguely familiar, but Brian couldn't place it. He switched off the radio and just lay on his back. He could make out the dark outline of the lampshades on the ceiling light. His parents used to have a similar arrangement hanging from their 1930s semi in Pinner... Then he suddenly sat up... The voice on the radio came back into his head. And now he recognised it. It was unmistakable. It was that mad genius. It was his comedy hero. It was the inimitable Peter Cook. He fell back on his pillow smiling and instantly fell into a very deep sleep.

———— ··●·· ————

Perhaps Magnus was right, thought Bernard. He'd always had a creative streak. Life might have been different if he'd had more understanding parents. His folks sounded as if they'd stepped out of the same stable as Angus's. But Angus had had the strength of character to show them two fingers. Unlike Angus, he'd always been too pliant, too much of the dutiful son.

Being an only child probably didn't help, and being gay - well, that made everything a million times worse. He hadn't had the courage to tell them about his sexuality until he'd finished university.

Switching courses had created the start of hostilities, but coming out felt like full-scale war. Neither of his parents had come to terms with the fact that they had a gay son. It was just too painful; too embarrassing; too far outside their comfort zone. That kind of thing just didn't happen to middle-class parents of their generation.

Still, he hadn't done too badly in the circumstances. He'd fallen into the advertising game by chance through his ex-boyfriend who had been a successful TV producer at JWT. He'd introduced him to Magnus at a party on a houseboat in Marlow, and they'd hit it off instantly. And he had Magnus to thank for getting him into the agency as a junior account handler. In just four years he'd managed to cement his place at the agency and now headed up the account team on one of the agency's most important accounts. It was a meteoric rise by any stretch of the imagination. His salary had escalated at an unreal pace and he was now fairly close to becoming a board member and an equity holder. He had sold his first property in East Finchley, a studio flat close to the tube, and exchanged it for a very lovely two-bedroom apartment carved out of a stunning Victorian edifice in one of Maida Vale's most desirable avenues overlooking the Regent's canal. And yet, his parents still had little to do with him. It was their loss, and there was absolutely nothing he could really do about it. But deep down, it pained him. In truth, it pained him a great deal more than he realised.

CHAPTER SIXTEEN

Angus slowly opened his eyes. The light was beginning to filter through the thick velvet curtains. She was no longer by his side but the bed was still warm where she had lain, and he could still detect her perfume on the sheets.

She was in the far corner of the room adjusting her hair in the mirror.

'Is it early?'

'It's almost seven... I suppose that's pretty early for you.' She came over to the bed and kissed him gently on the lips. 'Some of us have to work... Probably best if you discreetly head back to your room.'

'Yeah. Sure.' He picked up his clothes and wrapped himself in a bath gown that was hanging in the wardrobe. He turned to her. 'I'll see you at breakfast.'

'More than likely.'

'Great...' The coast was clear. He looked at her from the door. 'Oh... really nice etchings by the way.' Then he let himself out and closed the door gently behind him.

Bernard was the first to set foot in the breakfast room. He was usually an early riser. And was generally keen to embrace the elements first thing. This would usually take the form of a mile-long jog along the Regent's canal or a dip in the Highgate Men's Pond on Hampstead Heath. The Hampstead Heath swim was a very recent addition to his morning routine and was something he never thought he'd try. But Angus had bet him a tenner that he'd never have the guts to give it a go. Not being one to turn down a challenge, he'd gone and introduced himself to the members of Highgate Men's Pond one morning at 7.00 am and quite literally taken the plunge.

From that very first dip, he was addicted. Yes, it was bloody freezing, but once you became acclimatised, your body somehow adjusted and the feeling was just intoxicating and somehow rejuvenating. It was hard to put into words. But he knew from that very first experience that he was going to make this a regular routine. Aside from the experience itself, he really enjoyed the company of its members whom he had got to know very well.

There were men here of all ages including one of 87. And they were from such a diverse range of backgrounds. Mohammed was a middle-aged accountant working as a partner at Ernst & Young; Adrian was the 87-year-old and was a retired judge; Raymond was an East End tailor; Barry was a train driver on London's Northern Line; William was a young social worker from Hackney; and Harvey was a gay Anglican vicar. They were all such incredibly likeable individuals, and they'd all usually traipse off to Cafe Mozart in Swain's Lane afterwards for a chin-wag and a cappuccino. It was the best way to start the day, and he wouldn't want to miss it for the world.

'Good morning. Could I take your order for breakfast?' It was the attractive young girl with green eyes that Angus had taken a shine to.

'Good morning... Would it be possible to have a decaffeinated coffee and some toasted brown bread and marmalade, please?'

'Of course... No cooked breakfast?'

'No thank you. Tempting though it is.'

As she took his order back into the kitchen, other guests started to trickle into the breakfast room. Among them were Daniel Day, Hugh Digby, the woman with her hair in a bun who was in deep conversation with Jean-Pierre Barnaby, and a bleary-eyed Angus.

Angus pulled up a chair. 'Morning, Guv'nor. How are we this morning?'

'Good morning Shaggers... Reasonably bright-eyed and bushy-tailed I'd say... And yourself?'

'A bit shagged to be honest... Don't think we got much shut-eye... Not that I'm complaining. She's a bit drop-dead gorgeous don't you think?'

'Very lovely bone structure, I must say, and incredible eyes.'

'Aren't they just.'

Magnus and Brian now took their seats. 'Morning team. Trust we all, slept well, with the exception of Shaggers, of course.' They all chuckled, Angus included.

Brian helped himself to a piece of Bernard's toast. 'Heard a funny thing on the radio last night. I was nodding off to a phone-in and this bloke called Cederic from Cricklewood calls in and starts going on about the miners and what a filthy and vigorous job it is to do all that digging down the mines. Turns out he's a funeral director and knows all about the rigours of digging - and then he came out with a real killer... Says that he has a great deal of sympathy for the miners and that as a funeral director, he is no stranger to sympathy and coming over all sympathetic, which he says is an occupational hazard.' The others all chortled in unison. 'And then I recognised the voice... It was definitely Peter Cook. He was very funny. I'm not sure if the radio presenter knew it was him or not.'

Angus was well impressed. 'Wow… That's bloody fantastic… I'm sure you're right. The guy's a comic bloody genius. What a brilliant idea. Only Peter Cook could pull a stunt like that. Do you think he was pissed?'

'Quite possibly. But he was very coherent.'

'You said he was coherent that time when you helped him to his front door.'

'Yeah, he was. I've read that he frequently performs half-cut and still gets rave reviews, to the huge annoyance of Dudley Moore who has to carry him back to his dressing room.'

The table went silent as Sam arrived and took their orders. It was out of character for Angus to suddenly blush and go quiet. They smiled affectionately at each other as he ordered scrambled eggs. As soon as she had disappeared there was a terrible commotion out in the hallway where the dinner gong was being beaten frantically.

Bernard immediately got to his feet. 'I say, Commander. What the fuck's going on out there?' He made his way to the hallway where he found the aged and red-faced butler still frantically bashing the dinner gong like a maniac from the local lunatic asylum.

'Can I be of assistance?'

The old man stopped and looked up. Sweat was pouring off his forehead and he was out of breath.

'It's Lord Allard, sir… He's dead.'

CHAPTER SEVENTEEN

Detective Sergeant Arthur Bicknell had seen a fair number of murders in his time. But he'd never come across one in a pigpen. Though he had been reliably informed that it wasn't in fact a pigpen but a pen for wild boar. It was, needless to say, pretty bloody smelly and he had to watch where he stepped.

While his team quickly secured the area with police tape, he studied the body that was lying face down. A very cursory inspection led him to believe that the victim had received fatal wounds to both the torso and neck. But this, of course, was going to be the work of forensics who hadn't yet arrived on the scene.

He was just about to have a word with one of his team when he caught sight of something twinkling in the corner of his eye. It was protruding from the hay on the ground. He bent down and could see that it was a rather smart fountain pen and if he wasn't mistaken he could detect what looked like blood on the nib - unless its owner was in the habit of writing in red ink. He didn't want to touch it, even with latex gloves. He wasn't an expert on pens but knew that the distinctive white star motif on the top of the cap meant that it was almost certainly a Montblanc writing instrument. It may well have been the property of the deceased. If indeed it was the murder weapon, this case would undoubtedly go down as one of the strangest he'd come across and would be up there with the Charlie Craddock West Wittering murder. Craddock had been a small-time crook whose demise came about when he was drowned by having his entire head inserted into a goldfish bowl. He had actually swallowed a goldfish in the process.

In his own mind, he couldn't decide which was the most bizarre: drowning in a goldfish bowl or being stabbed to death with a fountain pen.

'Is that the murder weapon, sir?'

The young female officer had just located her boss inspecting the pen.

'It does look as if it may very well be precisely that, PC Winstanley. The forensic boys will know soon enough.'

He got to his feet.

'How many people are on-site, officer?'

'There are twenty visitors who stayed overnight, plus five members of staff. His two sons were here yesterday, but they returned home yesterday evening. The twenty visitors were all here for a marketing briefing apparently. Lord Allard is... was the CEO of Cranberry Crunch.'

'Good grief. No amount of clever advertising would get me to eat that muck. It's like eating bloody cardboard, isn't it?'

'Don't know Sir. I'm a muesli girl myself, Sir.'

'Good for you... Yes... Much more sensible... I suppose someone has to advertise the stuff though... Do you have a list there of everyone we need to interview, officer?'

'Yes Sir.' She handed him her list of everyone currently staying on the premises. 'Sir... Is it true that we will be trialling the new evidence recording system that the Home Office is thinking of implementing?'

'That's right I'm afraid. We'll be trialling it for the very first time with this case - God help us. The machines arrived this morning. Lots of bloody guidelines and paraphernalia. It's going to be a monumental pain in the arse... Christ knows what's wrong with a pen and notebook.'

As he spoke, the forensic team arrived fully kitted out.

'Morning Colin... Lovely day for it... The body is that of Lord Allard, and I noticed a fountain pen in the hay with what looks like traces of blood on the nib... so his nibs may very well have been murdered by one.'

Colin gave Arthur one of his quizzical expressions. 'I beg your pardon.'

'His nibs might have been killed by a nib.'

'Oh, I see... Very good. I'll have to remember that one... Not impossible, but not an easy thing to pull off.' Colin knelt carefully by the body and inspected it. 'You could be right though, Inspector. The carotid artery has been severed... He's been shot, too.' He carefully placed the fountain pen in a sealed evidence bag. On the cap, a name had been subtly engraved. It read: A. LOVEJOY. 'You might like to take a look at this, Inspector.' He held the bagged pen and Inspector Bicknell took a close look.

'Well, well... Very well spotted Colin.'

Colin smiled. 'We'll get on Inspector. Should have everything recorded by close of play.'

'Excellent Colin. Speak soon. We have a lot of interviews to get through.'

'Right you are Arthur... Who was it that said, "The pen is mightier than the sword?"'

'I'll have to pass on that one, Colin... But hang on one tick and I'll ask Officer Winstanley. She's a mine of information, that girl. It's an appropriate quotation in the circumstances... Very appropriate indeed.' PC Winstanley was with a colleague securing another piece of incident tape to one of the barn gates.

'Officer Winstanley! Can I trouble you for a mo?'

'Yes Sir.' She sidled up to him. 'How can I assist, Sir?'

'Seeing that you won the Christmas General Knowledge Quiz, I thought you might know the answer to a question that Colin here has just put to me.'

'Fire away Sir.'

'Who was it that said, ''The pen is mightier than the sword?'''

She giggled. 'That's an easy one, Sir.'

'Is it?... Well, it must have slipped my memory, which isn't what it used to be.'

'That quotation is attributed to the English author Edward Bulwer-Lytton and it comes from his play 'Richelieu' about Count Richelieu. You may well remember the quotation in full, Sir.'

'Might I?'

'True,—This!

Beneath the rule of men entirely great

The pen is mightier than the sword. Behold

The arch-enchanters wand!— itself a nothing!—

But taking sorcery from the master-hand

To paralyse the Caesars—and to strike

The loud earth breathless!—Take away the sword—

States can be saved without it.'

'Ah yes, Officer Winstanley... It's come flooding back to me. Thank you so much.'

'Pleasure, Sir... You'll have to excuse me now Sir. I have to make arrangements for the interviews.'

'Thank you, Officer...'

'She's got a fine brain, Arthur.'

'She certainly has Colin... I keep telling her she should go on bloody Mastermind. She'd win standing on her head.'

CHAPTER EIGHTEEN

———··●··———

'Ok, Officer Winstanley. You can press the green button on the cassette now.'

'Right, Sir.'

'Today is August 4th 1983. It is 11.00 am. We are in the drawing-room of Dingleberry Hall. I am Inspector Bicknell ID 76348. Also present is PC Winstanley ID 53728. We are interviewing Angus Lovejoy, date of birth 08.03.1959. Angus, can you confirm for the recording please that you are aware that this interview is being recorded?'

Angus coughed to clear his throat. 'Yes, I am aware that there is a pretty bog-standard cassette machine recording every word we say. And it doesn't appear to have Dolby.'

'Excellent. And, Angus, do you acknowledge that you were previously advised of your constitutional rights, that you signed a statement that detailed those rights and that you agreed to speak to us without having a solicitor present?'

'Yes, I can.'

'Can you tell us your movements as you remember them on the evening of August 3rd please, Angus?'

'No problem. At around 6.00 pm I went downstairs from my room to have dinner in the dining room. I was the third of our party to arrive. Magnus and Brian were already there. Bernard came down about 5 minutes later. I had pea soup followed by slices of meat and vegetables. I think the meat was wild boar, which we'd had for lunch, too. Very nice. I'd recommend it. Following pudding, which was apple pie and custard, we all went upstairs to play billiards. I took the others through the rules, and we all played. I beat everyone except Bernard. It was an excellent game, and he beat me by three points... Then I realised that I had agreed to meet with Sam at 8.00pm; she's the lovely waitress, and I was running a bit late. So I excused myself at about ten past eight.'

'Ok stop there please Angus.'

Arthur had been told by pathology that the death had occurred between 8.00 and 10.00pm. He had also learnt from Angus's working partner Brian that Angus possessed a Mont Blanc fountain pen. And it had been confirmed that the pen had been used to sever the carotid artery, and was one of two murder weapons. The other being a gun, which hadn't been found. There were no fingerprints on the pen other than Angus's, but there were very clear traces of dog saliva, And these matched samples taken from the only dog that resided on the estate - a sheepdog by the name of Oscar. So it looked as if the dog had picked up the pen and deposited it in the pigpen. Apparently, it had been known to steal food from the kitchen, which it also delivered to the wild boar.

'I am about to show Angus Lovejoy a photograph of exhibit A. Angus, do you recognise this Mont Blanc fountain pen?'

'Fuck me, yes... You found it. Brilliant!'

'So you think this is yours.'

'Well of course it is. It has my name engraved on the cap... I'm rather attached to it... It was a present from my mother actually... Writes beautifully... In fact, it was that pen that I used to write the line: Everyone Warms to a Real Fire. Can I have it back please?'

'You wrote those TV commercials, did you? Wow. They're brilliant. Better than some of the bloody programmes. They never fail to make the wife and I laugh. In fact, her indoors is now looking at getting a real fire installed. She's already had them down to sweep out the chimney...'

'Oh, thanks, Inspector. I created them with Brian. We are quite proud of them actually. I think we got a bit lucky, to be honest. The client has been brilliant.'

'That's terrific, Angus, Well done you... As for returning your pen, I'm afraid that won't be possible just yet...'

'That's ridiculous. Why on earth not?'

'Because Angus, I'm sorry to have to tell you that it was one of the two murder weapons employed to kill Lord Allard.'

'Shit!... That's probably gone and fucked up the nib then, hasn't it?'

'I don't know about the nib, but it certainly fucked up Lord Allard.'

'But that's preposterous. How can someone be killed by a bloody pen? Sounds like something out of Agatha Christie.'

'Well, I don't disagree with you there... It is a highly unusual use of a Mont Blanc pen. I grant you that.

'Getting back to the night in question, Angus. Can you confirm that you met up with Sam at ten past eight?'

'It was actually later than that.'

'Really? And how do you account for the time between leaving the billiard room and seeing Sam?'

'Well, it was on the way down to her room that I discovered that my beloved pen wasn't in my top inside jacket pocket. It's always clipped there, so I went in search of a member of staff... I found the housekeeper; a nice old dear. Her name is Joyce. And I reported to her that it had gone missing and she very kindly took all the details and said she'd keep an eye open for it.'

'And this Miss Joyce will be able to corroborate this?'

'Yes. I'm sure she will. Just ask her.'

'So what time did you meet Sam?'

'I guess it must have been close to half-past eight.'

'And how long were you with her?'

'All night... And yes, we did... And it was pretty bloody amazing if you must know... In fact, I think I might be head over heels in love, Inspector. It's never happened to me before. Been in love, that is. Do you remember when you first fell in love, Inspector?'

Inspector Bicknell went a little red. 'That was a long time ago, Angus... But yes, I do remember... You don't forget these things easily... It was at the village hall. We spotted each other across the dance floor. It sounds corny, I know, but I knew from the moment I cast eyes on her that I wanted to be with her for the rest of my life... And do you know, I can honestly say to you that we are still in love after all those years.'

Officer Winstanley had never heard the inspector speak so affectionately about anyone else before. 'That's lovely, Sir.'

'Well, she is a wonderful lady, my wife... I love her to bits...'

'I feel the same way about Sam, and I've only been with her for a night.'

'Well, you need to tell her how you feel...'

'Yeah... I know... you're right. But I'm terrified in case she doesn't feel the same way... And I don't want to lose her, Inspector.'

'That's life, Angus. Sometimes you just have to take that leap of faith... By the way, to change the subject, you said earlier that you thought this tape machine was a bit bog-standard.'

'Yeah, well it is... I mean it doesn't have Dolby noise reduction. And there's no editing facility or fancy stuff on it either.'

'You can edit tape can you?'

'Yeah, of course, you can... It's a bit tricky with cassettes but possible... When we go to sound studios to record radio commercials the guys spend hours editing the tape by physically splicing it. You can do it with razor blades.'

Officer Winstanley was rather worried that the tape machine was still running. 'Sir... Sir...'

'No please don't speak officer... this is interesting...

'So you can actually edit words out with a razor blade?'

'Yeah. It's dead easy. You need some special tape to join the tape together... It's a bit fiddly but very doable.'

'So you can edit words out that you don't want on there.'

'Piece of piss. Of course, it's easier to do it on reel to reel and then copy it onto cassette from the master... And with Dolby noise reduction, it will probably sound better than the crap reproduction on that thing...'

'Sir... Sir...'

'What is it, Winstanley? Can't it wait?'

'It's the tape machine, Sir... It's still running, Sir.'

'The tape machine's still running?... Oh, right... Of course, it is... Thank you, officer... Well, it is very interesting to know all that about editing, Angus... After all, we wouldn't want anything irregular happening to the tape recording, would we?... I think it's very good that we have recorded these concerns to alert the Home Office over possible future tampering with the machines. Thank you, Angus... I think we can end the recording now at 11.15.'

PC Winstanley pressed the red button and sighed a breath of relief.

'Nice one, Sir.'

'Thank you, Winstanley... Got a bit carried away there.'

'So Inspector, getting back to the matter in hand...', Angus picked up the photograph of his pen and studied it. 'What I want to know is why the fuck did anyone want to kill Allard in the first place? And why the hell do it with a stolen fountain pen?'

'Those are the precise questions running through my own head, Angus. But first things first. I'm going to have to speak to this Joyce woman and then to your Sam...'

'Her name is Samantha Pilkington...'

'Thank you... Once we have both their stories to corroborate yours, we can rule you out. And that's important because you are the owner of the murder weapon - at least one of them. And that alone makes you an immediate suspect.'

'Do you think Inspector that the person who stole my pen is the very same person who murdered Lord Allard?' asked Angus.

Inspector Bicknell scratched the stubble on his chin. 'I think it's a very strong possibility. A very strong possibility indeed.'

CHAPTER NINETEEN

—— ··●·· ——

Brian was feeling lazy this morning and took the lift. It was odd, he thought, that this three-storey building had one in the first place.

Angus had arrived before him for once. He usually rolled in at 10 o'clock and it was only 9.30.

'Morning guv'nor. Get an eye-full of this.' Angus had copies of the morning editions of the Sun and the Mail newspapers on his desk.

Brian removed his duffel coat and chucked it on the sofa, and then sat down to study the tabloids.

'Shit!' The front-page headline of the Sun was a classic screamer: ***WILL CEREAL MURDERER EVER DO PORRIDGE?***

There was a large photograph of Lord Allard and Dingleberry Hall on the front page with minimal copy.

Brian turned to the Mail and started reading the piece on its front page.

Lord Cecil Allard, Managing Director of Cranberry Crunch, the nation's favourite breakfast cereal, has been murdered with a fountain pen in mysterious circumstances at his country estate in the Cotswolds close to Chipping Campden.

Lord Cecil Allard who was a self-made multi-millionaire from humble origins, was murdered at his country seat in the idyllic Cotswold hills, according to Detective Inspector Arthur Bicknell who is heading up the inquiry into the murder.

"Lord Allard's body was found by the estate's butler Richard Haddock in the pigpen where Lord Allard breeds wild boar.

"He had been shot in the torso and stabbed in the neck with a Montblanc fountain pen," said Bicknell. "The pathology report," he continued, "concludes that Allard was fatally shot first and then stabbed in the neck with the pen."

There had been a party of 20 people staying at Dingleberry Hall who were taking part in a marketing conference set up by Lord Allard and his two sons.

Allard, who was the Managing Director of Cranberry Crunch, the nation's most popular breakfast cereal, was apparently in the process of reviewing the company's marketing, having suffered a string of disappointing sales results.

The Mail has learnt that all the occupants at the hall have now been interviewed by the police and while the majority had been discounted from their inquiries, there were a couple who were helping police with their inquiries and were being detained with the authority of a magistrate for up to 72 hours. We were also fortunate to speak to a number of the guests including Angus Lovejoy whose pen it was that was used as a murder weapon.

"I was originally seen as something of a suspect because of the pen," explained Lovejoy. "But the police soon realised that I was obviously an innocent party since I had reported that my pen had gone missing prior to the murder and could account for my movements during those critical hours when it is believed that Lord Allard was murdered."

Lovejoy is a copywriter at ad agency Gordon Deedes Rutter and was responsible for creating the much-talked-about advertising campaign for real fires.

Other guests who were in attendance included Ogden Baggott, the successful designer and founding partner of Baggott Associates. We asked him for his reactions to this dreadful and mysterious murder.

"The whole thing has been like a very bad dream," said Baggott. "I knew Lord Allard very well. We had been in talks for some considerable time about the future of his brand and I had liked him enormously. I just don't understand why someone would want to murder him and how they were able to do so without leaving any evidence at the scene of the crime. I am totally perplexed and upset by this whole thing. And I pass my sincerest condolences to the family at this incredibly difficult time."

The Mail was also able to speak to Hugh Digby whose sister is Allard's ex-wife.

"Of course, I was terribly shocked and saddened by this whole business," said Digby. "Despite my sister divorcing him three years ago, we had remained good friends. And I admired him. Admired him enormously."

Allard had, according to Digby, been the first person to introduce wild boar into the UK for breeding purposes, and had been supplying some of the most prestigious butchers, including Harrods, with his meat. While Cranberry Crunch had been his main source of income, the wild boar sideline had been a passionate hobby. "He knew more about wild boar than anyone else in this country," continued Digby, "and he won awards for his meat. His Wild Boar and Apple sausages were divine. But I don't suppose the business will continue now without his invaluable input."

There were pages of the stuff with photographs of all the guests including Brian's own mugshot, and a whole piece about the mysterious nature of the murder that speculated about how and by whom it could have been perpetrated.

'Christ! There are six pages of the stuff... And where on earth did they dig up that picture of me?'

'That's just the Mail, mate.' Angus recovered a stack of other publications that were under his desk. Look at this lot. And we've even made it into the New York Times - not the front cover mind you. Only page six - you can't have everything. He threw it over. The headline read in typical New York Times fashion: **LORD MEETS END OF PEN. STABBED WITH MONT BLANC; COPS BAFFLED**

Brian was about to take a look at The Times when his phone rang. He picked up the receiver.

'Morning. Brian here.'

'Morning Brian. It's Nicola. I have a call from your mother. Shall I put her through?'

'Thanks, Nicola. Yeah... I don't think I have a choice...'

'Brian.'

'Hi, mum. How are you and dad?'

'Never mind about me and dad. We've just seen your picture in the paper... Where did they get that one from? It's not one of your best, Brian. If they had come to us I could have given them a choice of lovely photos...'

'Yeah... I know mum. I don't know where they got it from. Some archive somewhere I suppose.'

'What a terrible thing to happen to that poor man though... Alright, so he bred pigs... Plenty of gentiles breed pigs... It doesn't make them targets for psychopathic murderers though, does it?'

'Actually, he bred wild boar, mum, and I don't think that was the reason someone murdered him.'

'Boar? Pig? They are all the same, Brian. They're filthy animals that roll around in mud all day. Not surprising we're not allowed to eat them. I'm sure they do untold damage to your insides... Anyway, do you think the police will catch the meshugenah that committed the crime?'

'I don't know mum. Apparently, the police have very little to go on.'

'And to kill someone with a pen... What kind of mishegas is that? I've never heard of such a thing. If you're going to murder someone, why would you choose a pen? A gun, a knife, or a bomb even. But a pen?'

'There was also a gun used, mum.'

'That I can understand... Anyway, your dad wants to say hello.'

'Our son the media star, how are you?'

'I'm fine dad, and yourself?'

'All the better for seeing your face in the paper - not that it was a nice story. Not nice at all... And they could have printed a better photo of you...'

'I know dad.'

'Did you receive the thermal vests?'

'Thanks, dad. Yes, I did. I meant to phone and thank you.' He hadn't even taken them out of the packaging.

'They are warm aren't they?'

'They are wonderful dad... I'm wearing them right now... I have two on actually.'

There was a pause. 'You don't want to put two on Brian... You'll be shvitzing in two. You'll overheat... Susan, he's put on two of those thermal vests.'

'He doesn't need two. One's enough. He doesn't want to get hot flushes at his age.'

'Dad... I have to go... I'll speak to you later.'

He put the receiver down and looked at Angus.

'You alright mate?'

'Yeah... Just the old fogies... They are lovely and all that, but they don't half drive me nuts.'

'At least they phone you and take an interest... Mine hardly speak to me. I get a birthday card every year with John Lewis vouchers and am invited for Christmas lunch every year, and that's about it. Don't think they've ever asked me about my work... They talk about Julian, my older brother all the bloody time. Julian and his glittering sodding career at the bar.'

'Which pub does he serve at?'

Angus laughed. 'If only... No, he serves as Queen's Counsel at Lincoln's Inn. And the sun apparently shines out of his proverbial.'

'Talking of sun shining out of one's proverbial, would you mind checking the fly shit on this press ad, chaps?' It was Pete from production with a proof of a press ad they had created for Barclays Bank. 'Fly shit' was the term coined for legal text that had to run at the bottom of press advertisements. It was referred to in these terms on account of the type being extremely small.

Brian took the proof. It was their first ad for Barclays and he was really pleased with it. The bank wanted to advertise the fact that they were investing large sums in sports facilities in deprived areas across the country, and Brian had come up with the headline: INVESTING IN FUTURES while showing a portrait of a young kid in a deprived area. To Angus's credit, he had loved the line and didn't want to change it. And Brian had got David Bailey to agree to take the shot of a young black boy in Dalston. It was a stunning shot.

While Brian checked the positioning of the fly shit, Bernard waltzed in with a copy of The Times. 'I take it you chaps have seen the papers.'

Brian put the Mail down on the desk. 'Angus has just enlightened me... Have you spoken to Magnus?'

'Not directly... I spoke to the police station earlier. Poor bugger is being detained for the maximum length of time - 72 hours apparently. They've got authority from the magistrate.'

'Fucking hell! That's outrageous. They know he was with us in the billiards room. We all told them.'

'I know Brian... I think they have to be seen to be doing something. And I don't know who else they've detained, but I get the distinct impression that they are clutching at straws.'

'What about his wife?' asked Angus.

'I've just been on the phone to her... She's in a right old state... Didn't know what to tell the kids... She can't even speak to him... I told her we were just going to have to sit this one out. I'm going over there tonight to cheer her up with teriyaki salmon, sauteed potatoes and mange tout.'

'Sounds very sophisticated. You're a good man, Bernard.'

'One tries... Look, the police don't have a shred of evidence against Magnus. So until the prodigal son returns, I suggest we carry on as usual. We're all grown up enough to approve our own work.'

Angus reached into his drawer and pulled out a key. 'And more importantly, we also have access to the most important filing cabinet in the agency.'

'Is that what I think it is?'

'It certainly is.'

'And has it been kept up to date, Angus?'

'It does appear to have been. When I last looked there were four cases of Stella Artois; two cases of Chateau Rothschild 1974; five cases of Bolinger; and four bottles of very good 25-year-old Balvenie Malt.'

'Sounds very respectable. I shall have to call you Commander.'

CHAPTER TWENTY

'I know I keep asking you this question Magnus, but it is vital that we know everything about your relationship with Tarquin Allard.'

'I wish you wouldn't use that word relationship. I'm not gay... As I keep telling you Inspector, I knew Tarquin from school days. We were quite good friends back in the day, and we bumped into each other about four years ago, and in an indirect kind of way, that's how the agency was invited to pitch for the business, which we subsequently won.'

'So did Tarquin tell you about his father's plans to review the account?'

'Yes, he did. I asked if we were about to be fired, and he said that we'd be invited to re-pitch. And I said that that sounded like a polite way of telling us to piss off, and he assured me that it wasn't.'

'And how do you think Tarquin felt about all this?'

'I don't think he was too happy... I think he was a bit embarrassed... He'd helped us win the business and was happy with our work. And he knew that the sales figures weren't down to the marketing. He wanted his father to look at other factors.'

'Other factors?'

'Yeah... You know, sugar levels, the ingredients, packaging - that kind of thing.'

'And Lord Allard wasn't interested in any of that?'

'No... I'm pretty sure he wasn't.'

'Did Tarquin ever discuss with you any plans to overrule his father?'

'No, not at all. Like everyone else, he was fairly terrified of the old bugger.'

'Am I right in thinking though that if it wasn't for Lord Allard, the account would look a great deal more secure for your agency?'

'That is true Inspector, but no sane person would contemplate murder. And I can assure you that I am perfectly sane.'

'Has Tarquin Allard ever discussed with you the possibility of taking over the reins from his father?'

'No, he hasn't.'

'Do you think Tarquin is an ambitious kind of person?'

'I don't think Tarquin is a schemer if that's what you are asking. I don't think he particularly wanted the job at his father's company as a matter of fact... He's a very talented artist, and it was his father who bulldozed him into working for the family business.'

'How bad would it be for your agency if you lost the Cranberry Crunch account?'

There was a pause. Magnus bit his lip.

'It would be pretty bad... It's our largest account... And it would take a lot of effort to replace the lost revenue with new business... It would probably lead to redundancies, and of course, it would make headline news in Campaign magazine, and that in itself can be damaging. So yes, Inspector, it wouldn't be great.'

Arthur Bicknell had pretty good intuition... He'd been thorough enough, but he knew that Magnus was telling the truth. They had absolutely nothing to go on. The only discernible motive among those present in the house was related to the business... The agency stood to gain in the event of Allard's death - as did the sons. But Bicknell's gut feeling was that this was a dead end. And his gut was invariably right - particularly when it came to murder.

'Ok - it is now 4.15 and this interview is terminating.'

Officer Winstanley turned off the cassette recorder.

———— ··●·· ————

Brian was sitting in his flat with his feet on the coffee table gazing at the ceiling. It was illogical, but for some unfathomable reason, he couldn't get that completely crazy thing his mother had said over the phone out of his head. She'd said something to the effect that if gentiles decided to breed pigs, that fact alone shouldn't make them targets for psychopaths.

It was totally nuts he knew, but maybe - just maybe in a roundabout kind of way, she was onto something. Everyone including the police had jumped to the conclusion that the murder had to be linked in some way to the Cranberry Crunch business. After all, it was worth a huge sum of money, and there were people at Dingleberry Hall on that fateful day who would clearly benefit from Allard's death. Namely, his two sons, and of course, Gordon Deedes Rutter.

But who might benefit if Allard's wild boar breeding and meat products were to suddenly cease? It wasn't by the look of it a particularly big business, but it probably had potential, and unlike Cranberry Crunch, there were no other competitors. Or were there?

Suddenly like a demented lunatic he ran outside and opened the metal dustbin. The bloody dustbin men were coming tomorrow. So he couldn't put it off. It wasn't going to be a pleasant job, but he'd just have to bite the bullet.

He emptied the entire contents that were tied up in plastic bags onto the driveway. It reeked something awful, and passers-by looked at him as if he had just been let out of the local looney bin. He then proceeded to untie the bags and remove every piece of revolting slimy garbage. There were chicken bones, fish bones, potato peelings, eggshells, tea bags, congealed pasta, mouldy vegetables and numerous other equally rancid objects to deal with. He spent the best part of an hour and was just about to give up, when he came across the precious item he was after. It was right at the bottom of one of the bags and it was stuck to an old sardine tin. Like everything else, it was wet, slimy and warm, but it was intact and it carried a rather nice illustration of a wild boar above which in bright red type were the words DIGBY WILD BOAR PIES.

• —— · •●• · —— •

Magnus badly needed to brush his teeth and shave. He felt like one of those down-and-outs sleeping in a doorway.

At least he'd spoken to Rebecca. She sounded so relieved to hear his voice and to know that he was in the clear. He was going to come home first, but she persuaded him otherwise. She was right, of course. He could go straight to the office via M&S for a change of clothes and an electric razor, and he'd be there in 20 minutes. If he came home now, he'd be writing off the entire morning.

Bernard had been a bloody saint. He owed him big time.

As he approached the concourse to King's Cross station, he found a telephone box and pulled back the heavy cast iron door, and nearly fainted. The smell of stale urine was intoxicating. It was too bad - he'd have to grin and bear it. He pulled out a load of coins from his pocket and dialled.

'Hello. Gordon Deedes Rutter. Can I help you?'

'Hi, Nicola. It's Magnus.'

'Magnus. My goodness... How are you? And where are you?'

'I'm fine thanks, Nicola. I've been released by the police. I'm a free man. I'm at King's Cross. Can you put me through to Penny please?'

'Of course. We'll see you shortly...'

'Magnus!'

'Hi hon...'

'Oh... It's so good to hear your voice... You poor thing... Is everything ok?'

'Yeah... Thank God. The police have released me. I think they've run out of questions... I'm coming straight in via M&S as I need a good wash, shave and change of clothes - not that you need to know all that. How have things been while I've been away?'

'Things have been fine, Magnus. But we've all been worried about you... How are Rebecca and the kids?'

'They are all fine and like all of us, relieved... Bernard was fantastic by the way. He went round there the other night with supper. Made them all laugh and took their minds off me.'

'Wow, that's so good of him... I had no idea...'

'Talking of which, could you book a table for him and me this afternoon at L'Escargot? I know he likes that place. It's the very least I can do.'

'No problem. I'll do it right away.'

———— ••●•• ————

Magnus showered and shaved in the agency's wetroom in the basement. It was the first time he'd ever used it since It was mainly used by all those sweaty bodies who risked life and limb by cycling in. He was pleased to see that it was well kitted out with plenty of quality Egyptian cotton towels and toiletries from Molton Brown.

Now that he felt human again, he made his way up the stairs to the creative department. The place seemed pretty quiet. Penny was at her desk, and as soon as she saw him she got to her feet and gave him a big hug.

'Welcome home you poor bugger.'

'Thanks, Pen. It's great to be back... Where is everyone?'

'Oh there's a director showing his showreel down in the boardroom... I've put your mail on your desk. Shall I bring you a black coffee?'

'Thanks, hon. You're the best.'

'Yeah, I know.'

He opened his office door and received the fright of his life.

The entire agency was inside and as soon as that door had opened, all hell broke out. There were party poppers pulled and champagne corks popped left, right and centre amid the strains of Elton John's recent hit *I'm Still Standing* throbbing through the sound system.

He'd barely set foot into the office when he felt the touch of familiar arms around his neck. He turned and was greeted by the lips of Rebecca. 'Welcome home stranger.' As they kissed there was spontaneous applause followed by the tapping of a spoon on a champagne flute.

Kenneth was standing on a chair. 'Now I know the past few days have been bizarrely surreal and stressful, but I'd just like to say a few words... Magnus mate... welcome home. I can't tell you how relieved we all are to have you back. This whole episode has obviously been traumatic for all of us - particularly for you and Rebecca and the kids - as well as the Allard family, and I have already spoken to both Tarquin and Mark and passed on the agency's sincerest condolences. Like Magnus, they, too, have until now been held in police custody. I have only just got off the phone to Tarquin who is obviously in a state of shock. To lose one's father in these circumstances is bad enough, but to be regarded by the police as a potential suspect must be awful beyond words... But as far as we know, the police have now eliminated from their inquiries all those staying at the house on that fateful day. And if the newspaper reports are to be believed, the police investigation is now struggling to conduct its inquiries in light of the dearth of any tangible evidence... Anyway, that aside, I can also tell you that Tarquin, bless him, was very open and candid on the phone just now... I wasn't going to broach the subject of business for obvious reasons, but he brought it up himself... And he assured me that under his and his brother's stewardship the Cranberry Crunch business will no longer be placing its marketing activity under review and that the new design guidelines drawn up by Ogden Baggott won't be applied to our advertising activity. So in this respect, we can all take a huge sigh of relief. For us, at least, this particular grey cloud clearly has something of a silver lining...'

There were a few more champagne bottles popped and spontaneous cheers.

'So now, without further ado, I'm just going to let Magnus say a few words if indeed he so wishes.'

'Thanks, Kenneth. He knows me so well... I'm not one to turn down the chance to open my gob in public... Well... those last couple of days were interesting... if a little Kafkaesque... As an agency, we've had plenty of campaigns snuffed out by clients over the years. But this is the first time the client himself has been terminated and quite literally shelved in a fridge. But sadly, unlike many of our shelved campaigns, Lord Allard can't be resurrected to live another day. And that of course is desperately sad for the Allard family to whom we send our deepest condolences. As for the police, what can I tell you? Well, their accommodation isn't great, and Penny, you'll be relieved to know that the coffee down the nick wasn't a patch on yours. But in fairness to them, they were courteous and were doing their job to the best of their ability, and for that I applaud them. This investigation will, I suspect, continue for some considerable time. Reports in the media, as Kenneth has already said, imply that there is very little hard evidence for them to go on. And I feel for the police because they are under the most intense pressure to solve this crime. But seriously, this experience has made me realise that I'm one lucky bugger... To have one loving family is a blessing, but to have two is something else. I will never take you guys for granted. Thank you. I love you all. And now, I'd like to get a little bit tipsy and urge you all to do likewise. And if any of you find this course of action irresponsible, I'd just like to draw your attention to the words of one of our greatest statesmen Winston Churchill who when told that he was drunk by a female MP replied with the following words: "Madam, you are ugly. But tomorrow I shall be sober and you will still be ugly.'"

———— ··●·· ————

L'Escargot had established itself as one of the finest French restaurants in London. Housed in a splendid Georgian townhouse dating from 1741, it had once been the home of the Duke of Portland.

Magnus always insisted on the same table in the corner by the window. He liked seeing the world go by while enjoying fine cuisine and good company.

'Cheers Commander.' Bernard sipped his glass of Château de Pommard. He loved this place even if it was the same room in which his ex had informed him six months ago of their impending breakup.

'I don't know about you, Bernard but I'm going to plump for the fricassee of snails, wild mushrooms and foie gras followed by cassoulet Maison à la façon du chef.' The waiter nodded dutifully and turned to Bernard.

'I will copy my colleague here and also have the snails to start, please. And I'll follow it with the baked lobster with garlic butter and a side dish of pommes dauphinoise and spinach, thank you.' The waiter collected the menus and returned briskly to the kitchen. Bernard poured more wine into Magnus's glass. 'I always feel compelled to have snails to start here... Nothing quite like them.'

'Funny isn't it... the whole idea of putting slimy garden insects anywhere near your mouth is repulsive, and yet here we are taking delight in doing just that.'

'That's the magic of French cuisine for you... Apparently one of the early owners of this place had a snail farm in the basement.'

'How very enterprising... Rearing your own livestock on the premises... The only other place I know that does that is Jimmy's Greek restaurant on Frith Street. Trouble is there are no culinary uses for cockroaches.'

'Don't knock Jimmy's... That place is an institution... Ok, it's a bit grubby...'

'A bit? They keep the lighting really low just to hide the greasy smears on the tablecloths. The place is crawling...'

'It's certainly crawling... usually with inebriated creatives.'

'You're not wrong there, Bernard... I'm afraid I count myself among them... And you're right about it being an institution - just an incredibly grubby one… But don't get me wrong. I am as fond of that grubby little hole as you are, and I wouldn't want it to smarten up its act. There's something about the place that sums up the indomitable spirit of Soho.'

'I'm with you on that one, Commander…' Bernard raised his glass. 'Here's to the indomitable spirit of Soho.' They both quaffed their wine and savoured the moment. 'So, to completely change the subject, do you have any theories about who might have murdered our client?'

Magnus placed his glass on the tablecloth and twiddled with the glass stem. 'I'm about as baffled as the police. I don't think they ever thought Angus was a serious suspect even before they received the lab report about dog saliva on the pen and his water-tight shagging alibi… And to be fair, they only held me because of that telephone conversation I'd had with Tarquin and the fact that we knew each other from the past; that and his obvious disagreement with his father over the company's marketing strategy. I suppose the police saw a potential motive between the two of us; some clandestine scheme to wrestle the business from the old man… But the poor sods had nothing else to go on… To be honest, I think they're out of their depth here… Whoever did this knew how to cover their tracks… I reckon we're dealing with serious organised crime… But then again, what do I know? Perhaps we'll never know the truth.'

Bernard nodded. 'Well, it's kept the papers pretty busy. This story and the endless speculation over the Lord who was stabbed to death with a fountain pen in a pigsty has certainly captured the public imagination. And we've received an extraordinary amount of free publicity as a result. Even the bloody Solids have benefited from it… Geoff called me yesterday. He was like a dog with two dicks over the fact that five national newspapers had mentioned in their reporting of the case that Gordon Deedes Rutter was the agency behind the real fires campaign. He reckons that alone has probably given him half a million quid's worth of free media space... So you're absolutely right about silver linings and all that - but one doesn't want to make too much of it... Feels like dancing on poor Allard's grave.'

'Abso-bloody-lutely... Poor sod... He might have been a grumpy and curmudgeonly old bugger, but he didn't deserve that... It's funny though how something as dreadful as this can lead to positive stuff for us at any rate.'

'Don't imagine our friend Mr Baggott will be too pleased to learn that Tarquin won't be implementing his grand plan.'

'I hadn't given that irritating little weasel of a man a moment's thought. But I daresay you're right... Do you think he'll come up with a corporate design manual for the funeral service and cortege?'

'I can see it now... A 500-page document on the use of sympathetic typefaces. And the stipulation of certain appropriate black and dark grey shades - not to mention the tone of voice guidelines that rule out the gratuitous use of humour.'

The waiter arrived with their starters - snails in garlic butter served in specially designed dishes with several round dimples for said snails and a small fork with which to extract them.

'Did you ever have any dealings with Allard senior, Magnus?'

'Hardly... As you know, he was rarely wheeled out and was something of a puppet master, pulling all the strings behind the scenes. I think he came to the agency on one occasion but didn't stay very long... Excused himself on the grounds of having to meet someone very senior at Harrods... No - he left the boys to do all the heavy lifting... Kenneth knew him better. He'd had meetings with him at the house. I only spoke to him twice... Once when he came into the agency, and last year at the British TV Awards... Actually sat next to him.'

'Oh, what joy.'

'Quite... The conversation revolved around wild boar. He was apparently the first person in the UK to breed the bleeders and won prizes for them. He was quite keen to share his extensive knowledge about breeding the bloody things. Called them porkers. I think he was more interested in those animals than he was in the breakfast cereal... Of course, muggins here feigned interest, as one does. But with the best will in the world, it's pretty difficult to keep a straight face when you're being given graphic details about the best methods to achieve successful impregnation of female wild boar.'

'Blimey... That's enough to put you off your Spotted Dick...'

'You're telling me.'

CHAPTER TWENTY-ONE

'Feel free to tell me that I'm completely bonkers, but have a look at that.' Brian put the label that he'd discovered in his bin in front of Angus.

'DIGBY WILD BOAR PIES... Are these something to do with Allard?'

'I don't think so... But look at the name... Ring any bells?'

'I've heard of cowbells, but wild boar bells... Hang on... Wasn't that strange cove at the Dingleberry ding-dong called Digby... Hugh Digby... Diggers to his friends if memory serves...'

'Precisely... And he seemed to take an interest in Allard's wild boar.'

'Yes... Strange bloke... Something a bit creepy about him, I thought... Do you reckon he's the same Digby behind Digby Wild Boar Pies?'

'It's a bit of a long shot, I know. But I've been to the reference library and looked up the company by rifling through their telephone directories and Yellow Pages. And guess what... the company's registered address is in the Cotswolds and it's the same address as his residential listing.'

'Blimey Finklebrain, you have been busy... If it is the very same Digby, I suppose that could make him Allard's competitor in a very niche market.'

'That's exactly what I thought.'

'It's one thing to be a competitor... but a murderer?... That's one hell of a jump, isn't it?'

'I know... It's a bit far-fetched. But it's slightly odd that he didn't mention his business over lunch... Just seems fishy to me. And bumping off Allard might have been some kind of motive.'

'I suppose it's just possible. But he just didn't seem like the murdering sort to me.'

'I'm sure they said that about Dr Crippen. But what does the murdering sort look like anyway?'

'I guess I had a neanderthal psychopath in mind... So what are you going to do?'

'Well, I thought I should go to the police...'

'Hang on... I'm not so sure that's going to work... From my experience, I don't think they'll take this very seriously...'

'What makes you think that?'

'Two reasons... Firstly, I don't think they're much cop... Sorry, that wasn't meant to be a pun. They're just a bit crap. And secondly, they're not going to take kindly to some poncy, jumped-up advertising kid coming up with a theory based on a pork pie wrapper.'

'So what do you suggest? Just forget about it?'

'No... I'm not suggesting that at all... I'm as intrigued as you are... Look, I've promised to take Sam somewhere for the weekend... Why don't we all just go to the Cotswolds and do a recce of Digby's gaffe? I'll drive... We could even knock on his door on the pretext of asking for some water for the car, and then act all surprised when we recognise him... What do you say?'

'Sounds like a plan... Will Sam be up for it?'

'Would have thought so... She's just like me in that respect. She has the adventurous streak... And I'm sure she wouldn't say no to staying in a five-star jobbie with a luxury spa... Not to mention a choice of characterful watering holes.'

'You should be a bloody copywriter... I'm sold!'

———— · ·•●·· ————

'Magnus. I have a Donald Clegg on the line from the D&AD.'

Magnus was feeling a little worse for wear as the effects of the Château de Pommard and those earlier G&Ts were conspiring to make everything a bit blurred and indistinct, but the mere mention of D&AD brought him to his senses.

D&AD was the Designers and Art Directors Association of the United Kingdom - one of the most prestigious and well-respected advertising awards bodies in the world.

'Hello. Magnus speaking.'

'Good afternoon, Mr O'Shea. My name is Donald Clegg and I'm calling from the D&AD... And I'm very pleased to be able to tell you that I have some very good news to impart...' There was a little cough and Magnus could hear pieces of paper being shuffled at the other end. 'Yes, I can tell you that Gordon Deedes Rutter has received three awards this year for its client the Solid Fuel Advisory Service. These awards are in the Television category. And I can also tell you without actually going into specifics that one of these awards is very significant indeed. So you will no doubt want to prepare your dinner jackets and book tables in advance... There is an 'Early Bird' discount for advanced bookings.'

'That's wonderful news. The award that is - not the Early Bird dooh-dah... Not that the Early Bird thingummy isn't good news... Thank you very much.'

'It's my pleasure, Mr O'Shea. And on behalf of D&AD, I would like to extend our hearty congratulations to you and your team... It's a wonderful campaign, and a very worthy winner.'

There was a click and the line went dead. Magnus put the phone down. He really wasn't feeling too good at all. He pulled himself out of his chair and worked his way down the corridor and stumbled into Angus and Brian's office, both of whom looked up in surprise.

'Sorry chaps to butt in like this unannounced... Some bad news I'm afraid... We're going to have to open the drinks cabinet again.'

———— ·•●•· ————

Brian was just unloading the dishwasher when the sleek chocolate brown open-top Mercedes slid into the parking space outside. Within a few seconds, Angus was hooting. The neighbours weren't going to appreciate having their peace so rudely broken by some dip-stick in a Mercedes on Saturday morning while enjoying their cornflakes to the dulcet tones of Roy Plomley's Desert Island Discs on Radio 4.

Brian kicked on his shoes and let himself out of the ground-floor flat. Angus was sporting Ray-Bans and a leather bomber jacket and Sam sat next to him in a fetching green tartan jacket.

'Love the car luv. When did you pick it up?'

Angus propped his sunglasses on his head and turned off the ignition. 'Picked her up yesterday. She's a real beauty, isn't she? Current company excluded.' Sam nudged him in the ribs, and he placed his arm around her shoulder. 'This will be our first proper trip in her. She's six years old and has barely 20,000 on the clock... Drives like a dream and flies like shit off a shovel on the motorway... When are you going to get yourself a set of wheels, Brian?'

'I'd better take the test first.'

Angus chuckled. 'Yeah... I was forgetting... That would help... Look, why don't you chuck your stuff in the boot and hop in the back?'

The light tan leather upholstery was impressive and had that very distinctive and rather pleasant aroma. Angus was right. She was a real beauty. Almost as beautiful as the creature that sat in the passenger seat in the front.

———— ·•●•· ————

Angus drew up opposite the Grade II Regency facade of the Cotswold House Hotel in Chipping Campden. It was a stunningly attractive example of a Cotswold high street hewn from that golden limestone that typifies Cotswold architecture.

Angus opened the boot and removed their luggage. 'I bet this place has had its fair share of period film shoots.'

Brian squinted through his glasses and raised a hand to shield his eyes from the afternoon sunshine. 'Yeah, it's pretty perfect save for the cars, yellow lines and signposts. Nice little job for the retouchers, though.' Brian had become only too familiar with the twilight world of retouching. It was an incredibly skilled and specialist service that all the leading advertising agencies spent a fortune on to make their clients' products look their very best. Banks of skilled retouchers would spend endless hours working with the assistance of magnifying glasses, fine brushes and special dyes and bleaches to enhance 8x10 negatives as well as prints. There were only a handful of really good retouching studios in London and they coined it like nobody's business. Of all the industry suppliers, it was the retouching studios that threw some of the best and most lavish Christmas parties and sent out the most expensive Christmas presents in the form of vintage wines. They could afford to.

'Good afternoon, and welcome to the Cotswold House Hotel. Would you like to check in?' The girl behind the elegant reception desk was equally elegant and had clearly gone for the Lady Diana hair thing.

'Thank you. It's Angus and Sam Lovejoy and Brian Finkle.'

'Ah, yes... Here we are. You have the superior double and the executive single - rooms 5 and 9 respectively. Did you have a pleasant journey from London?'

'Yes, thank you. The traffic wasn't too bad.'

She handed them the keys. 'Your rooms are on the first floor. Dinner is served in the dining room between 6.30 and 8.30 and breakfast between 7.30 and 9.30. Would you like to have your bags carried up?'

'No that's fine thanks.' He turned to Brian. 'I suggest we reconvene at the bar in half an hour.'

<hr />

'He seems very sweet.'

'He's a good egg is our Brian. But he could do with a good woman.'

'Am I a good woman?'

'You are more than a good woman.'

'Am I now?'

'And am I a good man?'

'No, Angus Lovejoy, you are not a good man. You are a very naughty man... Now, shall we try the bed?'

'What a very good idea.'

She pushed him mischievously onto the king-size four-poster and switched off the light.

'We've only got half an hour.'

'Well, that's fifteen minutes more than you usually take.'

Brian ordered a Southern Comfort and a bowl of peanuts from the bar. He had an inkling that they'd be late down. He'd got to know his partner in crime pretty well. He was like a dog on heat. Mind you, he couldn't blame him. Sam was rather lovely and the pair of them couldn't help keeping their hands off each other.

He'd almost finished the nuts by the time they materialised.

'Sorry, we're a bit late Brian. Can I get you another one mate?'

'Thanks that would be nice. Southern Comfort, please.'

Sam sat next to Brian. 'So how long have you lived in Hampstead?'

'No time at all. Just a month. It's my first property.'

'Wow... Nice place to get your foot on the property ladder... I know it well. I was brought up in Hampstead.'

'Really? I had no idea.'

'Yeah. Do you know Burgh House?'

'Yes, of course. I've been to their cafe in the basement. They do really good homemade brownies.'

Sam laughed and flashed those green eyes. 'I know them only too well. They are great, aren't they? Well, anyway my parents used to have a house very close in Well Walk.'

'They no longer there?'

'No. They divorced when I was fifteen and sold the house. But I still have fond memories of the place... Angus said you met Peter Cook when he'd had a few too many.'

'Yeah... I helped him into his house. Turns out he lives round the corner in Perrin's Walk with a Chinese girlfriend who is a lot younger than him... Funnily enough, his house backs onto a convent, which seems rather appropriate for someone who's been known to dress as a nun.'

'That is funny.'

'Angus says you are at art college.'

'Yep... I'm a struggling penniless artist at Chelsea School of Art... I'm living in a friend's spare room nearby in Jubilee Place off the King's Road for a peppercorn rent. I'm really lucky.'

'Sounds really cool.'

'Yeah, it is actually. It's my friend's parents' house. Her parents spend half the year at their other place in the South of France and it's such a big house that they don't really notice little old me... You'll have to come over. I'll introduce you to Louise. She's really nice...'

'I'd like that.'

Agnus returned with the drinks. 'Cheers, everyone. Here's to our little adventure.'

Sam raised her gin and tonic. 'Our little adventure.'

'So Brian, when do you think we should pay our Mr Digby a visit?'

'There's no hurry. I wouldn't mind pottering round the village and taking a look at that antique market across the road... Why don't we seek him out after breakfast tomorrow?'

'Sounds like a good plan... Well, this place is rather nice, I must say... I wonder if they have wild boar on the menu.'

CHAPTER TWENTY-TWO

'Magnus, I have Susan Cox from Campaign Magazine on the line for you.'

'Thanks, hon, do you want to put her through?'

'Sure thing...'

'Hi there Susan... Long time, no speak.'

'Good to hear your voice, Magnus... Sorry to hear all about this dreadful murder and your terrible ordeal.'

'Thanks, but it wasn't that much of an ordeal for me... It's the Allards I feel most sorry for.'

'Quite... It doesn't sound like the police are getting very far.'

'No... They seem to be completely stumped by the whole thing. It's all rather surreal, to be honest.'

'I'm sure it is... And it's partly why I called... You see, we'd like to run a feature piece about this whole episode, as well as your latest campaign for real fires... It's a lovely campaign by the way, and is the talk of the town right now... I don't know how you got Brian Clough to sit with Don Revie on the sofa like that. But it's bloody funny... '

'That's very kind of you Susan. I'd love to help in any way I can.'

'Well, ideally I'd like to interview you about the whole Lord Allard thing and also get Angus Lovejoy's perspective on it... seeing that he was also questioned by the police and that one of the murder weapons belonged to him... Did he ever get his pen back by the way?'

'That's a very good question, Susan... I don't think he did. Bit of a shame... He was rather attached to it. I think it had been a birthday present... I'm sure Angus would be only too happy to oblige.'

'When would be a good time to talk to you guys?... Ideally, we'd like to run this piece in a couple of weeks.'

'Angus and his art director Brian Finkle are away for a few days. Why don't I get him to call you back? They were the creative team behind the real fire campaign, so you'll probably want to speak to both of them.'

'That would be fantastic. Thank you so much, Magnus. I really appreciate that.'

'No problem. Speak soon.' He put the phone down.

Those two boys were making waves... They were fast becoming the agency's most valuable asset in the creative department. They'd almost certainly have headhunters calling them up and enticing them with more money. If he was going to retain them, he was going to have to persuade Kenneth that they were a worthwhile investment - sooner rather than later.

— · •●• · —

The roof blinds in the old orangery were down this morning to filter out the morning sunshine and protect its guests and its other inhabitants - the tropical palms and giant cacti. It was a lovely setting for breakfast, and the views of the garden reminded Sam of her parents' garden in Hampstead; its manicured lawn that her father took such pride in; the herbaceous borders with their showy displays; and the one-hundred-year-old magnolia tree that looked so magnificent in full bloom until its large saucer-shaped pink petals cascaded to the grass after no more than a two-week appearance.

'Shall I be mother?' She stirred the teapot and poured it into Brian's cup. 'I think we should head off straight after breakfast... What do you reckon?'

Angus looked up from the breakfast menu. 'Yeah... No time like the present... Actually, I've given it a bit of thought... We should get the bonnet of the car up and while Brian and I stick our heads into the engine, you Sam should probably knock on his door and ask politely for water for the engine... Well, he's not going to say no to a pretty young damsel in distress, is he?... Sorry, Sam, I assume you're ok with that.'

'That's fine. I do a good damsel in distress. Look...' She then gave them a particularly flustered look and they all started to laugh.

'That's very good... And once he has responded to your plea for help, I'll pop my head out of the bonnet and express my surprise at recognising Diggers,' added Angus. 'I'm sure he'll ask us all in for tea... He's that kind of bloke.'

'What kind of bloke is that, then? The murdering kind?' quipped Sam.

Angus winced. 'Cruel but fair... I take your point... We obviously don't know much about the bugger... Brian, you talked to him far longer than we did. What's your assessment Doctor Finklebrain?'

Brian pulled his glasses down his nose. 'Vell my analysis of ze patient known here as Diggers is somesing of a mixed bog. On ze von hend ve hef a classic case of, how you say, delusional behaviour - of a man who sinks he is loved by everyone and on ze ozer hand ve hef someone who likes to shoot and stab people in ze neck.'

'Well, thank you for that riveting analysis Dr Finklebrain.' Angus stretched for the teapot. 'Shall I be mother figure?'

They all chuckled and a couple of the other guests looked on in disapproval. This wasn't the kind of place for young noisy whippersnappers from London to disturb the peace. They clearly had far too much money to splash around at their age and were no doubt part of the burgeoning and vulgar entertainment world. This kind of thing was systemic and represented the gradual erosion of the establishment in the name of 'progress' that had all started with the seemingly innocuous appearance of newscasters on the BBC with quirky regional accents.

———— ··•·· ————

It was an incredibly pretty drive to Blockley. The address that Brian had found was a detached house on the High Street. Like all the other properties in the area, it was hewn from the golden Cotswold limestone and looked reasonably old if simple in its squarish design. A dainty Regency porch complete with climbing roses and an elegant leaded roof framed the front door. Angus pulled into the side of the road directly in front of the house where they were in full view of the occupants and released the bonnet by fiddling with a device below the dashboard.

'Right… Are we ready to do this?'

Sam and Brian were about to respond but were distracted by the sound of three police cars suddenly arriving on the scene from the opposite direction. Two parked in front and one behind and a number of policemen emerged and knocked at the door while a few others went round the back by negotiating the hedgerow.

Hugh Digby answered the door, all smiles. One of the officers flashed what Angus thought was a warrant card, and Digby was led to the parked car and immediately whisked away. Other officers were in the house and were presumably looking for incriminating evidence.

Angus scratched his unshaven chin and sucked in air. 'Looks like we won't be needing any water for the car, after all... The police aren't quite as stupid as I thought.'

CHAPTER TWENTY-THREE

'Alright, Officer Winstanley. Would you like to press the green button on the cassette now?'

'Right, Sir.'

'Today is August 10th 1983. It is 11.00 am. I am Inspector Bicknell ID 76348. Also present is PC Winstanley ID 53728. We are interviewing Hugh Digby, date of birth 22.06.1939. Mr Digby, can you confirm please for the recording that you are aware that this interview is being recorded?'

Hugh smiled cheerfully. 'Yes, I have been informed by Inspector Bicknell here that this conversation is being recorded as part of a trial programme for the Home Office.'

'Excellent. And, Mr Digby, do you acknowledge that you were previously advised of your constitutional rights, that you signed a statement that detailed those rights and that you agreed to speak to us today with your solicitor Mr Arnold Davis?'

'Yes, I do acknowledge that.'

'Mr Digby, when originally questioned at Dingleberry Hall on August 3rd, you told us that you spent the entire duration of the evening at Dingleberry Hall on that fateful evening in your bedroom reading... Do you stand by that?'

'Yes... I do.'

'Well, that's interesting... because we have just been told by the housekeeper Ms Joyce Carrington that she forgot to mention that she did see you leaving Mr Allard's office before turning in for the night, and she always goes to bed at 9.30. Ms Carrington suffers with the early onset of memory loss but she knows that it was definitely the evening in question because she had just been listening to her favourite radio broadcast 'Letter From America' by Alistair Cook. She even outlined to us the content of that broadcast, which concerned itself with the political careers of Margaret Thatcher and Ronald Reagan. We have checked this out by referring to the Radio Times, and this does seem to be correct. Actually, I do listen to Mr Cook myself from time to time, but annoyingly I missed that particular broadcast, which is a shame.' There was much whispering between Mr Digby and his solicitor. 'Mr Digby. Do you still stand by your account of your movements, or lack of movements on the night in question?'

Hugh Digby was now looking less than his cheerful self. 'I decline to say anything for fear of incriminating myself.'

'We have also looked into your financial affairs, Mr Digby and it seems that you also have a business that involves rearing wild boar. Is that correct, Mr Digby?'

Hugh Digby nodded.

'For the record, Mr Digby is nodding. Would you like to confirm this verbally please Mr Digby?'

'Yes, this is true.'

'Would you say then that you are a business competitor of your brother-in-law's?'

Hugh Digby's solicitor once more leaned over and whispered into Hugh Digby's ear.

'On the advice of my solicitor, I decline to comment for fear of incriminating myself.'

'And can I ask you Mr Digby if your brother-in-law was aware of your own wild boar breeding activities?'

Further whispering ensued. 'I cannot make any comments, Inspector.'

'I am now showing Mr Digby a photograph of a hand-gun... Do you recognise this photograph, Mr Digby?'

Hugh Digby nodded.

'Mr Digby is nodding. Would you like to confirm that for the recording?'

'Yes... It's my damn gun... And, no I did not use it to shoot my brother-in-law!'

'I wasn't suggesting for one moment that you did... But you obviously have an interest in guns and know how to use them... I assume you have a licence for it.'

Inspector Bicknell knew that this gun wasn't the murder weapon. Forensics had already established the kind of gun and calibre used, neither of which matched this one.

'Yes, of course... I have it in my safe...'

'And why do you possess a gun, Mr Digby?'

'I am a member of the National Rifle Association, Inspector, and take part in the annual pistol shooting competition. It's a sport, Inspector; one that I enjoy a great deal.'

'And do you have access to other guns, Mr Digby?'

'As a matter of fact, I do. I possess a shotgun and a rifle. The shotgun is for clay pigeon shooting, and the rifle is also used for competitions run by the National Rifle Association.'

'How long have you been in business with Digby Wild Boar Pies, Mr Digby?'

Hugh Digby was relieved that the inspector had now moved away from the subject of guns. He didn't like talking about them as a general rule. And he knew it would only be a matter of time before people would put two and two together - particularly the police - and blithely assume that he had something to do with his brother-in-law's demise simply because he had access to guns.

'I set up the business just over two years ago.'

'I'm impressed, Mr Digby... I sampled one of your pies earlier today... Quite delicious if I may say so... I think you've gained a loyal customer.'

Hugh Digby smiled with some pride. 'Oh, that's very kind of you, Inspector...'

'Not at all, Mr Digby... I am rather partial to pork pies. But I have to say that your wild boar offering is in another league altogether. I don't think I shall look at another pork pie in quite the same way.' The two men laughed and the atmosphere became a little less tense. 'Tell me Mr Digby, was your brother-in-law helpful when you set up your business?'

'To be honest, he was extremely helpful, Inspector... He imparted a great deal of information about rearing wild boar. I don't suppose he'd have been quite as forthcoming had he known that I was going to set up my own business. But to begin with, I didn't even know myself that I was going to do so... It just kind of happened... Like you, Inspector I was blown away by the taste and texture of the product... I suppose it became something of an obsession...'

'How very interesting, Mr Digby. I think we will pause here. The time is 11.15. Would you like to stop the recording, Officer Winstanley?'

Arthur Bicknell didn't want to push Digby too hard. He was going to take his time. He seemed like a complicated character. Nothing quite made sense and he was clearly holding something back. The inspector had no reason to disbelieve the housekeeper's statement about Digby leaving Allard's office just before turning in at 9.30. Had Allard been in the room with him? Had something occurred in that office that made Digby want to shoot his brother-in-law? These were clearly crucial questions. And it wasn't beyond the realms of possibility that this mild-mannered eccentric did, in fact, shoot his brother-in-law in cold blood. He'd seen stranger things. Far, far stranger. As far as he could make out, Digby was the only person in the house other than the two sons and the incumbent ad agency that had anything to gain from Allard's demise. But the sons and the agency could all account for their movements and were happy and at ease to be interviewed without a solicitor. The two sons had left the house at around 7.00 and had spent the evening with their wives. They had both been in shock. And that look of shock is something you can't actually fake. Lovejoy had spent the night in bed with the girl. And the advertising boys Finkle, O'Shea and Hamilton had stayed together after the billiards until midnight at the local pub The Fox and Hounds. Their stories all tallied and there were plenty of witnesses in the pub. Digby was the only one who seemed to have something to hide.

——— · • ● • · ———

He was feeling surprisingly calm in the circumstances. Though he was beginning to feel that he shouldn't have listened to the bloody solicitor.

At the end of the day, Diggers old boy, you just have to do what feels right. It was his motto. Still, that Inspector Bicknell seemed like a decent enough old cove. And fancy him saying all that stuff about his pies... The man had taste and he'd gone up inestimably in his estimation. Now, that was a nifty form of words, he thought... Something those advertising boys would no doubt enjoy. Perhaps he was missing his vocation. But on second thoughts, perhaps that wasn't something he'd have relished. Deadlines and all that wouldn't have appealed; and the thought of working on second-rate products like frozen chicken nuggets or boil-in-the-bag curries or British Leyland cars - well, the mind just boggled, didn't it?

• —————— · •●• · —————— •

'So, do you really think this Digby character could have shot and stabbed old Allard with my fountain pen, which incidentally I still haven't had returned by the police?'

Sam made a face. 'Do you really want it back? I mean, doesn't it give you the willies?'

'The willies?... Don't think I've ever experienced those... You'll need to talk to Bernard about that. He's had a fair few in his time...'

Sam nudged him in the ribs. 'Poor Bernard... Don't be rude about his sexual orientation.'

'Yeah... it's rude,' added Brian. 'It's below the belt.'

'About four inches below the belt, I'd say... But seriously, do you think he is capable of such a crime?'

Brian looked thoughtful. 'I think anyone is capable of committing murder given the right set of circumstances... But the honest answer to your question is I don't know... I wonder how long they'll hold him for.'

'They can hold him for up to five days,' said Sam.

'She's not just a pretty face...' Angus ran his hand through her silky hair. 'Didn't know you were a bit of a legal expert on the quiet.'

'I'm not... It's just that I had an uncle who was always getting into trouble with the police, and he was once held for five days, and I remember my father saying that that was the maximum detention time the police could hold him without charging him.'

'Five bloody days... That's a long time... I hope his wild boars don't go without their dinner for five days.'

'I can see the headlines now, ' chipped in Brian. 'Wild boars starved by the pigs.'

'Very good, Brian. Do you want a job as a copywriter?'

'No thanks... I'll stick to drawing and colouring-in... less taxing on the brain... And anyway, I've already got a copywriter bloke that does that for me some of the time... when he isn't looking at scantily-clad girls through his telescope or reading The Times.'

'Sounds like a bloke after my own heart...'

'And who might these scantily-clad girls be?' Sam looked a bit hurt.

'Well, actually it's only one girl - and she's hardly a girl. She's the local prosie... The agency's in Soho, don't forget.'

'And you have a telescope in your office just to spy on her?...'

'It's not mine... It belonged to the depraved soul that used to occupy the office next door... He was fired for fiddling expenses and nicking a board-room table... So we just nicked his telescope.'

'To be fair, Sam, Angus hasn't been spying on her of late... I think the therapy sessions have really been helpful...'

There was a pause, and then all three of them started to get the giggles.

'You two don't know how lucky you are... You get paid silly money to be silly - full-time.'

'Yeah, you're not wrong, Sam, it is a silly industry,' admitted Angus. 'But being really good at being silly takes a great deal of serious dedication.' He wasn't being entirely flippant for once. Both he and Brian had worked hard at honing their craft, and it was a craft that the UK had begun to dominate. This small island produced some of the world's finest creative advertising thanks to its healthy crop of talented copywriters, art directors, commercial directors, and photographers. Many of its leading exponents had made the seamless transition to the worlds of literature and feature films and risen to the top of those industries, too. People like Fay Weldon, Salman Rushdie, Peter Mayle, Alan Parker, Hugh Hudson, David Putnam, Ridley Scott... But it hadn't always been like that. The birth of creative advertising had kicked off in the 60s in New York, and one Bill Bernbach was perhaps one of its greatest pioneers. It had taken this country a couple of decades to take note, catch up, and make its presence felt.

'Talking of murder... I could murder a pint right now, followed by a chicken Tikka Massala and poppadoms.'

'Now that sounds like the best idea you've had all week.'

'Thanks a bunch.'

'My pleasure... There's a lovely-looking curry house just down the road. Why don't we go for a quick sherbet at the King's Head and then check it out?'

Brian grinned. 'Sounds like the best idea you've had all month.'

———— ··●·· ————

Susan had a soft spot for this place. She loved the agency's work and Magnus was a lovely guy; funny, self-deprecating, talented, and good-looking to boot. It was a shame he was already married. But there was something else she liked about the place... It wasn't pretentious like so many other agencies. Everything about it down to the slightly faded decor was endearingly appealing to her. There weren't any fancy atriums; nor were there acres of black polished wood and high-end Italian office furniture. They could easily have given the place a facelift ages ago but had clearly chosen to focus on its creative output instead. For a small agency, it punched well above its weight and had won all the major awards including as many Cannes Golds and D&AD pencils you could shake a stick at. It was also the only agency in town that was bonkers enough to have a reception area that was basically a very large sandpit replete with deckchairs and the sound effects of waves lapping against the shore wafting through the sound system. It was nuts, but like everything Gordon Deedes Rutter produced, it was memorable.

'Susan... You can go up now. Angus and Brian are back from their meeting. Their office is third on the left, next to Magnus's.'

'Thanks, Penny.'

If anything, the creative floor was even tattier than the rest of the building. She tapped on the door that was half-closed.

'Enter, if you're feeling brave... Oh, hello... I'm Angus. You must be Susan from Campaign Magazine.'

'Yes... That's right.'

'Do come in Susan... This is Brian by the way.'

Brian looked up from his desk where he had been busy on a layout for a new soft drink launch.

'Hi, Susan. Why don't you take a pew next to the telescope?'

Susan removed a box of magic markers and sat on the couch.

'So how long have you two worked here?'

Brian looked at Angus. 'Christ - that's a good question. Seems like forever but we've been here no more than six months.'

'Wow. That's amazing... So much has happened since you've been here.'

'You can say that again,' said Angus. 'I mean, one occasionally hears of clients being fired, but never shot.'

'It has been surreal, hasn't it? Something of a rude awakening for you guys... But what an incredible start you've had with that fabulous campaign for real fires... Am I right in thinking that this was your first brief?'

'Yeah, we were both teamed up by Magnus, and thanks to him we were given a chance to have a stab at the brief... Oops, no sick pun intended... Magnus was working on it, too.'

'Did Magnus have a script of his own, then?'

Brian and Angus laughed at the question. 'That's a really good question, Susan... Thing is, Brian and I have never really got to the bottom of that one... Magnus just loved our campaign and got behind it. He never showed us anything he'd come up with.'

'That's what we really like about the culture of this place,' added Brian. 'It's all about getting the best ideas through the system, and it doesn't matter who comes up with them... Some creative directors want to do all the work and won't give junior teams like us a chance, but Magnus isn't like that, and it's testament to him that this agency has won so many awards.'

As Brian and Angus spoke, Susan jotted down notes in her notebook.

'Actually, Susan, why don't we continue this conversation over coffee?' suggested Angus.

'And if it's a long piece you're after, we could stretch it to lunch,' added Brian. 'Do you like Italian? Only there's a fab little place in Greek Street that does a cannelloni to die for.'

'I'm actually after two feature pieces, so we may need dinner as well. Have you two been to Langan's yet?'

Brian and Angus looked slightly mystified. 'Should we have?' asked Angus.

'Oh yes... It's most definitely the place to be seen. It's where all the big dicks in this industry hang out... Let me book a table for 7.00... You'll love it. And besides, it won't do your careers any harm to be seen in the company of a senior reporter for Campaign. It might even get a few tongues wagging.'

CHAPTER TWENTY-FOUR

———··●··———

Giuseppe Esposito was tired. It had been a particularly good year for harvesting the olives. The 10 hectares had been in the family for four generations. He may have been the 70-year-old owner of the estate, but that wasn't going to stop him from rolling up his sleeves and taking part in the harvest. Ever since he'd been a small child in short trousers he'd done so, and he was going to continue for as long as his ageing body would let him. Admittedly, this year had been more exhausting than previous years, and the slow onset of osteoarthritis in his left knee hadn't helped matters.

He slumped wearily into the leather seat of his Alfa Romeo and started the ignition. He was looking forward to the weekend. His three children and their respective families were making their annual pilgrimage to the family home and Maria had prepared their favourite dishes: Risotto Alla Milanese and Ribollita.

He eased the gearstick into fourth gear and snaked his way through the verdant hills that were Campania towards the ancient city of Sessa Aurunca where he'd pick up a case of decent local wine from Pietro.

No more than ten minutes into the journey, he could see that a tree had fallen across the road ahead. He slowed the car. A feeling of foreboding possessed him. Giuseppe was shrewd. Ever since the anonymous death threats, he had been careful and taken precautions. The car had been discreetly armour plated and been specially fitted with bullet-proof glass. His worst suspicions were beginning to come to fruition as a red car appeared in his rearview mirror. He did a sudden u-turn and floored the accelerator. Within seconds the car was sailing like the wind at 100 miles per hour. As he passed the red car, he felt the bullets ricochet off the car body's steel plates and the passenger seat's window shattered but stayed in place. Giorgo's glass had performed well. The needle had now touched 130. He knew the terrain like the back of his hand and swerved off the road down a dirt track. The tyres surprisingly hadn't been hit. God was with him as he tore at speed through the dense undergrowth. He was on Giovanni's smallholding and was in two minds. He could continue for another half mile down the farm track to the nearest tarmacked road or he could head for the disused barn. The track down to the road provided little cover, so he instinctively sped towards the barn. Once inside, he pulled himself out of the car. The exterior body panels had been peppered with bullet holes. Had they known about the armour plating, they'd have gone for the tyres. He opened the boot and removed the gun. It was a pretty old Heckler & Koch MP5 submachine gun, but it was good enough to give the bastards hell if need be. He closed the two large swing gates and secured them with a long timber beam, and then surveyed the road through a rust hole in the corrugated wall. They were taking their time, but he eventually spied the red car and its accomplice heading his way and kicking up red dust in their wake. He felt the trigger against his finger and readied himself to give them a deadly burst. Thankfully, it wasn't going to be necessary. They carried on towards the main road and were soon out of his field of vision. But he wasn't going to move until he was sure that they wouldn't return. He'd wait here until the light faded and make his way back to the estate in the dark.

CHAPTER TWENTY-FIVE

The red Lancier swerved and stopped by the tarmacked road. There was no sign of the prick in the Alfa Romeo. The road was deserted in both directions. How had they failed to eliminate the bastard? They'd sprayed him good and proper from the passenger side. Antonio thumped the steering wheel in annoyance.

'Merda! Merda! Quel bastardo è scappato. Torniamo indietro.'

He turned to Alberto in the back seat who was removing the magazine from the gun. 'We head back now, boss?'

'Sì... Yes... We head back now.'

Alberto opened the window and gesticulated to the other car.

Both cars stopped before two imposing iron gates. Alberto got out and opened a steel security box with his key and punched in a code and then relocked the security box. The iron gates slowly swept open and the two cars continued on the private road for about half a mile through olive groves.

Casa Desolata was a Renaissance pile that had once been owned by Lorenzo de' Medici

The cars pulled into the forecourt and Antonio ripped off his sunglasses and jogged up the mansion's steps. Two bodyguards in black suits and polo necks let him through into the marble-clad entrance lobby that dripped with gold leaf and oil paintings including a recently acquired Giotto and Donatello. Antonio headed for the library; it was where Luca, his father, spent most of his waking hours these days. Another bodyguard let him through the large walnut doors into the magnificent library with its stunning frescoes and enormous collection of antiquarian books.

Luca Brambilla was in his usual place, sitting behind his desk overlooking the gardens. He had his reading glasses on and was engrossed in one of his calf-bound first editions. His father had always insisted that his boys addressed him in English. It was a pain in the arse for Antonio. But in the grand scheme of things, it was a small price to pay. His father had a thing about the English. He loved English culture; the pomp of its Royal Family; Rolls Royce motorcars; and Charles Dickens. He prided himself on having read the great man's works in both English and Italian translation, and his impressive library boasted five shelves of the novelist's complete works in their pristine first-edition calf-bound volumes. He even named the fucking place after one of that English mother-fucker's books. Casa Desolata - Bleak fucking House.

Luca Brambilla had seen it all: abject poverty as a child and untold wealth as an adult. Aside from being cultured, Luca was smart. He'd always been one step ahead of the competition.

'So, the prodigal son returns... Tell me, how did you get on with our Signor Esposito?'

'He's a slippery fish, papa... We hit him hard. Very hard... I don't know how the bastard got away. But he did... I'm sorry...'

His father rose from his desk and removed his reading glasses. He placed his hands on Antonio's broad shoulders, kissed him on his forehead and took his son in his arms. 'It is probably for the best... He may be a thorn in our side, Antonio, but the man isn't a bad man... Besides, he also has a large family.'

Antonio didn't understand his father at times. 'But papa... How can you say that? What he is campaigning for will ruin our plans for the future... We can't let him do that.'

Luca looked at his son compassionately. 'In life, you have to learn to respect your enemies, Antonio. So please don't call him a bastard... Did you know that our Signor Esposito raised 4 billion Lira last year for homeless children?'

Antonio shook his head.

'As I say, he is a good man, and I never feel good about spilling the blood of a good man - and nor should you... No, what you did will suffice... It will send him a message. Now that he knows how we feel; that we mean business, he'll have the chance to back off. Let's see if he heeds your warning... Don't look so downcast. Sit here. Let me read you this passage.'

Antonio smiled and sat in the armchair on the other side of the desk.

His father picked up his book and placed his reading glasses on his nose. 'Pride is one of the seven deadly sins; but it cannot be the pride of a mother in her children, for that is a compound of two cardinal virtues - faith and hope.'

Their mother had died only a year ago and the pain of her absence was still keenly felt. The quote was beautiful. And it had been for her.

————— · •●• · —————

Giuseppe tapped lightly on the glass panel of Giovanni's back door. He had decided to leave the car in the barn and make it by foot to the farmhouse.

Giovanni opened the door. 'Ah, Giuseppe. È buono vederti.' The two men hugged.

Giovanni removed a bottle of chianti from the wine rack and poured two generous glasses. Within minutes Giuseppe was telling his friend about his encounter and how close he had come to death. Following a hearty lasagne, Giovanni and his five sons accompanied their friend to the barn armed with shotguns. Giuseppe was like a brother to his friend and there was nothing he wouldn't do to help him. They would all stay with him tonight and stay on guard. They were all in this together. The Brambilla family had taken things to a new level, but they weren't going to be bullied. Their livelihoods were at stake. If the Brambillas were going to play dirty, so would they.

————— · •●• · —————

Rafael had been a butler to the family for well over twenty years. Signor Brambilla had originally taken him in as an orphan. He'd fed and clothed him; he'd educated him, and now here he was as Head Butler - responsible for running the household. It was a job and a half. He was charged with managing the accounts and hiring and firing all the domestic house staff. When you included the gardeners, that was close to 150 individuals. It was like running a medium-sized business. Thankfully, the house's security arrangements weren't his remit - he had enough on his plate. He was good at his job, and in return, he was well looked after. Besides being well paid, he had his own apartment and was to all intents and purposes, a member of the family.

Today was clearly going to be a big day. All five sons and their respective families were going to be here for the weekend. Signor Brambilla had summoned a family meeting. Veal was on the menu and the finest vintages from the cellar were being lined up. There was clearly going to be some kind of big announcement. Perhaps, Signor Brambilla was going to hand over the reins to one of his sons. Naturally, Rafael was keen to know himself what was afoot. After all, if Senior Brambilla was standing down, his own future might be put in jeopardy. While he had an affinity with the old man, there was no such relationship with the sons.

Rafael stood by the kitchen window polishing one of the lead crystal glasses as the first of the weekend's guests arrived. It looked like Tosca the lawyer with his glamorous wife and two children. The dark blue Saab parked next to Antonio's Lancia and the family spilled out, led by the two young boys who raced each other up the steps shouting, 'Papa, papa!'

———— ··●·· ————

Family occasions were usually held in the Blue Dining Room, which was one of the less formal rooms in the house. It had been where the sons had always eaten as children with their mother and a succession of nannies.

The fact that Signor Brambilla had instructed him two days beforehand to prepare the State Room had alerted Rafael to the gravity of today's proceedings. The room hadn't been used since the Brambillas' Golden

Wedding Anniversary dinner four years ago. It was a magnificent room that could seat 50 guests very comfortably around its vast mahogany dining table. So today it looked rather strange to see the table prepared for just eleven places.

The grandchildren of whom there were 13 had been catered for on the terrace and were being entertained by a magician and balloon artist.

Rafael felt honoured to be included in the proceedings and had been seated next to Signor Brambilla. He had shared small talk with all five sons before taking their seats. Tosca had been his usual cold self. He never asked after Rafael and only ever spoke about his legal practice in Florence. Carlo was far warmer and always embraced Rafael like a brother. He was the business brains of the family and was often to be seen with Signor Brambilla in the old man's office. He was, in Rafael's mind, the most likely successor, as he clearly had more dealings with the family business and was the apple of his father's eye. Fabio was the most distant and bohemian of the boys, and Rafael had the distinct impression that he had a certain disdain for the family business. He was a very talented classical pianist and composer and his wife was a cellist and had occasionally performed recitals at the house. Luigi was the one son he had seen least of all. He ran a successful restaurant business in Naples and was apparently in negotiations with a production company in Milan to produce a series of cookery programmes. Then, of course, there was Antonio who was the only unmarried son and the only one to live on the premises. He was moody, impetuous and nothing like the others, but he clearly doted on his father; and Signor Brambilla seemed to have a soft spot for him.

During the main course, Signor Brambilla turned to him. 'Rafael, you have excelled yourself. The veal is outstanding.'

'Grazie... Thank you, Signor. I will pass your compliments to the chef... He was a wonderful find... Trained, I believe in Rome.'

The old man nodded. 'We are indeed fortunate to have him with us... Rafael, tell me... are you happy?'

Rafael was taken aback by the question. Signor Brambilla had always been nothing but kind to him, but he hadn't ever enquired in such a personal fashion after his wellbeing. 'Yes, Signor, I think so.'

'It's just that I don't want you to feel like a prisoner in this place... I am proud of you, Rafael, you know... And I want you to be happy...'

'Thank you, Signor...'

'I don't wish to pry, but should you ever wish to raise a family of your own, I would be more than happy for you to do so here... I would have no objection... No objection at all... We have the space... And well, this place is perfect for the sound of tiny feet. You could always take a couple of the master bedrooms upstairs and convert another one into a living space.'

Rafael was astonished. Had Signor Brambilla known about Sofia? He couldn't have, but somehow the old man's intuition had kicked in. 'That is very kind of you, Signor... As it happens there is someone in my life...'

Luca Brambilla smiled warmly and raised his glass. 'I'm so pleased for you, Rafael... May I enquire what her name is?'

'Sofia.'

'Well, if at any point, you'd like Sofia to live here, just let me know and I will make all the necessary arrangements.'

'Thank you, Signor Brambilla. That is so very kind of you.'

'And what may I ask does Sofia do in terms of work?'

'She's a teacher.'

'Excellent. The noblest of professions... To nurture young impressionable minds...'

There was a clinking of glass as Carlo got to his feet.

'Dearest Papa... Firstly, on behalf of the whole family, I would like to thank you for having us all here today and for laying on such a fabulous meal in this extraordinarily beautiful room. A room in which I had the pleasure of dancing with our remarkable and beautiful mother four years ago... Now, as you all know, Papa and I have been steering this business through turbulent times over the past couple of years and we have finally come to the conclusion that now is the right time to embrace change. In many ways, the future is looking very exciting for us, and the reason Papa has called this meeting is to outline to you all in some detail the new business model that Papa and I are now proposing. So without further ado, I would like to invite Papa to take the floor... But before doing so, could I ask the ladies please to retire to the drawing-room for tea and coffee and something rather exotic prepared by Luigi? And Rafael, would you mind accompanying the ladies please?'

Rafael's heart sank. He was being excluded. So he wouldn't get to hear any of the details concerning the business. But it didn't sound like Signor Brambilla was stepping down. He smiled, placed his napkin on the table and led the ladies to the drawing-room.

CHAPTER TWENTY-SIX

It was a pretty country church just outside Oxford, and it was about as full as it could get.

Magnus, Bernard, Angus and Brian sat in pews three rows from the family, and the vicar was in full flow.

'Lord Cecil Arthur Allard was born in Whitechapel in the East End of London in 1910 to Colin and Susan Allard. He was their only child and was much loved. Indeed, Cecil would speak fondly of his childhood, despite its obvious hardships. His mother was an amateur singer and his father a tailor, and work at that time was patchy, to say the least. And it was against this humble background that the young Cecil would make his mark in this world. He was clearly a very bright child and easily gained a place at grammar school from where he won a place at Trinity College Cambridge to read Classics. But it was, of course, his natural skills as an entrepreneur that we remember him for. On leaving university, he set up his first business - a classic car dealership Marque of Distinction, which famously leased vintage cars to film productions. He eventually sold the company in 1970 and founded Cranberry Crunch from a small warehouse near St Albans. Under his stewardship, the company went from strength to strength and in as little as five years, became a public listed company. Today Cranberry Crunch is the nation's favourite breakfast cereal. But of course, his greatest pride and joy was his successful wild boar breeding programme. He was, in fact, the first man in this country to breed wild boar and was immensely proud of that fact. Indeed, I think he was more proud of that achievement than being appointed a Life Peer in 1974 by the queen on the advice of Harold Wilson, the then Prime Minister. His marriage to Melanie, which produced two sons, dissolved amicably in 1979. And it is a credit to Lord Allard that Mark and Tarquin have managed to keep the business on an even keel during these very difficult times.

'Lord Allard's life was in many ways an extraordinary and inspirational one that reflected the 'rags to riches' tales of his great childhood hero Charles Dickens whose novels he had read as a small boy. "Dickens," he said, in an interview for the Sunday Times, "was my saviour. Without Dickens, I wouldn't have had the wherewithal and sheer determination to overcome adversity." And so it is that we learn today that Lord Allard has left a significant sum in his will to the Dickens Society.

'Lord Allard's life will have touched many of us, and I for one shall miss him terribly. May God bless Lord Cecil Allard, and may he rest in eternal peace.'

Magnus turned to Brian. 'Blimey. I had no idea that he came from such a humble background. I always thought he was posh through and through.'

Angus smiled. 'Works the other way, too... I knew someone at school whose father was one of the richest men in the country. But it didn't stop the son from dropping out and living in a squat.'

By the time they arrived at Dingleberry Hall, the sun had decided to make an appearance.

About half of those who were in attendance at the church were now standing in small clusters on the terrace with plates of crustless sandwiches and cups of tea.

Angus spotted Hugh Digby and nudged Brian who was in mid-conversation with Sam.

'Sorry to butt in, but look who's just arrived - 2 o'clock.'

Brian and Sam looked up. 'My word... I didn't see him in the church.'

'Nor did I... I'm going to say hello.' And with that Angus was off.

Hugh seemed very relieved to see someone he knew.

'Hello there Angus... Very nice to see you again, albeit in very sad circumstances.'

'Likewise, Hugh... I didn't see you at the service.'

'No, I'm afraid I wasn't able to make it in time... I've only just arrived.'

There was a slightly awkward silence.

'To be honest, Angus, I have had the most stressful few days.'

'Oh, I'm sorry to hear that, Hugh. Can I get you a cup of tea and a sarnie?'

'That's very kind. I could murder a couple of sarnies.'

'Sure thing.' As long as he didn't want to murder anyone, too into the bargain, that would be hunky-dory.

Angus strolled into the orangery where a long table had been set up for tea, plates of sandwiches and other nicely prepared comestibles. He was served by a young girl who offered him a cup of tea and a plate of dainty ham sandwiches.

By the time he returned, Hugh was already talking to Sam and Brian.

'Here you go, squire. This should hopefully fill the hole.'

'Thanks a million, Angus.'

'Pleasure... So what has been causing you so much stress of late?'

'I've just been telling your colleagues here - boring them rotten, I'm sure.'

'Well, you can bore me rotten, too if you like.'

'I've been held by the police for the past five days... They thought I had something to do with my brother-in-law's murder... And it took five sodding days to convince them that they were barking up the wrong bloody tree.'

Angus feigned surprise. 'So what made them think you were the murderer?'

'There were a couple of things that made them suspicious... I hadn't been forthcoming about my wild boar breeding activity.'

'Wow. I didn't know you bred those, too,' lied Angus.

'No, there's no reason why you should have. I generally don't advertise the fact... Actually, Brian here has tried one of my wild boar pies. And I'm delighted to say that he really enjoyed it.'

'Yeah it was bloody lovely - and that's coming from a Jewish pork pie connoisseur,' added Brian.

'Anyway, they thought that I was a competitor of Cecil's,' continued Hugh. 'Which I suppose I was, really. They also knew that I had access to guns. But I think the thing that really got their goat was the fact that I had been economical with the truth vis-à-vis my movements on that fateful night... I had originally told them that I had spent the entire evening reading in my room... But then the housekeeper came forward and had remembered seeing me come out of Cecil's office and had informed the police. Had I told them about all this from the outset, I wouldn't have been detained. So it's probably my own stupid fault... Mind you, my bloody solicitor didn't help matters much by telling me not to answer half the questions for fear of incriminating myself.' He wolfed down a ham sandwich.

'So you were with Lord Allard in his study?' Brian inquired nonchalantly.

'I was... Cecil wasn't a happy bunny... He had heard that I had been in conversation with Harrods about stocking my pies, and he was not in the least bit happy about it... Said I had been a conniving wotsit by going behind his back... and that I was undermining his own relationship with the store... He was actually pretty furious. So I said that I was going back to my room to let him calm down and that we'd continue the conversation when he was in a better frame of mind... Well, that was the last time I saw him alive, wasn't it?'

'I assume the police have now eliminated you from their enquiries,' added Angus.

'I'm hoping so. They haven't said as much, but they seem to accept everything I've told them, albeit grudgingly... It took them long enough though... Funny thing is, I don't want to go through with the Harrods thing now... out of respect for Cecil... Just feels wrong. Can you understand that?'

All three of them nodded. 'I think that's a perfectly normal reaction in the circumstances,' said Sam.

'Yes, I suppose it is... Anyway, that's enough about me. How are you all doing? And tell me, what was the outcome of that meeting? I imagine it's all been put on hold now...'

'We're all fine thanks', replied Brian cheerfully. 'And as far as we know, Tarquin and Mark have canned the idea of reviewing the account. To be honest I don't think the two boys were keen on the idea in the first place.'

'Is that right?... I'm not surprised. Cecil was an extraordinary chap, but he could be bloody difficult and stubborn at times. I think that's why my sister left him.'

'I had no idea that he was from such a humble background,' added Brian. 'My grandparents were Jewish refugees from Russia and they settled in Whitechapel. Incredible to think that they may have rubbed shoulders with Lord Allard's parents.'

'It is indeed a funny old world.'

Brian was now feeling a tad guilty about suspecting Hugh Digby of murdering his brother-in-law. It had been a fairly hair-brained theory, in retrospect, and he now felt stupid for having delved into his dustbin for the wild boar wrapper.

'Tell you what,' said Hugh. 'Why don't you chaps come down to my place for a weekend?'

Angus and Sam immediately made positive noises. 'That would be really lovely, wouldn't it, Angus?' said Sam, and Angus agreed enthusiastically.

'How about you, Brian?'

'That would be very nice. But are you sure you'd like us reprobates to disturb your peace?'

'Absolutely... The place is too damn peaceful if the truth be known. It would be my pleasure to have some extra company... And there's a jolly good watering hole within staggering distance.'

'Now you're talking,' added Angus. 'Do you have a vacancy for three reprobates next weekend?'

'Let me just check my bookings book.' He reached into his jacket pocket and pulled out a little red diary and flicked through it extravagantly. 'Well, that's lucky. I have vacancies for the next 48 weeks.'

CHAPTER TWENTY-SEVEN

— ·•●•· —

Giuseppe and Giovanni both possessed gun licences for personal protection, having served for many years on the Antimafia Commission. They and their colleagues had certainly made some progress with tightening regulations and putting away some very dangerous individuals. But in truth, the Commission had only scratched the surface. Organised crime in Italy continued to soar, and many good men like Giuseppe and Giovanni had lost their lives to the mob. More disturbingly, there were signs that the mafia was diversifying and becoming far more sophisticated in its operation.

The Brambilla family was a case in point. Luca Brambilla was a criminal genius and had accumulated vast sums through criminal activities that even the Commission couldn't get to the bottom of. But what was becoming evident was that the Brambilla family's activities under the direction of Luca Brambilla were now moving into the world of agriculture. It was, of course, a brilliant move for several reasons. Agriculture on the surface seemed like a very unlikely and unsuspicious place for any criminal activity, and also a relatively safe place to launder money. But more ingeniously,

Luca Brambillaba had found a way to make it incredibly profitable.

As landowners themselves, Giuseppe and Giovanni had discovered that huge swathes of cheap land were being leased by third parties on behalf of the Brambilla family. At first, the two men were mystified by this. Why would the family want to lease so much land? But after careful detection work, they discovered the reason.

Luca Brambilla was leasing land in order to claim the European Economic Community's farming subsidies. And the family was claiming these subsidies without, in many cases, even farming the land. It was a clever scam, and it was making the family more money than drug running, racketeering and prostitution put together. And, of course, it was a great deal safer.

So Giuseppe had begun campaigning for stricter lease holding controls to clamp down on these irregular practices. In doing so, he knew that this would draw the ire of the family, but he was prepared and taking precautions - his armour-plated car being just one of those safeguards.

Giovanni had also, with the assistance of his sons and officials at Milan Airport, been monitoring the activities of some members of the family, particularly Antonio who had been travelling to the UK.

They now knew that Antonio had flown to London recently and was flying there again today, and had booked a couple of rooms at a hotel in a place called Chipping Campden. They didn't know the purpose of these flights but they were sure that they would have been connected to the Brambilla business model in some shape or form. With any luck, Antonio would lead them to an answer.

CHAPTER TWENTY-EIGHT

———— ··●·· ————

'Good morning. The time is 9 O'clock. This is Brian Redhead. You are listening to The Today Programme on BBC Radio Four. Here are the headlines: Defence Secretary Michael Heseltine is making a surprise visit to British members of the Lebanon Peacekeeping Force... In the bizarre murder investigation of Lord Allard who was found in a pigpen having been shot and stabbed with a fountain pen, a fourth suspect has been released by the police... And the Irish Prime Minister Dr Garret Fitzgerald has called for greater cooperation between Britain and Ireland in the fight against terrorism. With details of these stories, here's our newsreader Philip Hyman.'

Brian's ears suddenly pricked up. 'Do you want to turn the volume up, Sam?'

'Sure.' She stretched forward and fiddled with the volume knob, as Angus pulled into a layby, and the three of them listened intently.

'The Defence Secretary Michael Heseltine is today paying a surprise visit to the British contingent of the multinational peacekeeping force in Beirut. It's the first time he's been to Lebanon as Defence Secretary - flying in by helicopter from Cyprus. The troops he's gone to see form the smallest part of the peacekeeping force. There have been calls for them to be withdrawn after attacks on the American and French contingents. But the government is firm that the one hundred or so men should remain.

'Here at home, a fourth suspect held by police over the murder of Lord Allard has been released. The murder of Lord Allard has been one of the most bizarre and baffling murder investigations in recent years. Having been shot and stabbed with a fountain pen on his own estate, the police inquiry has struggled to gain headway due to a dearth of forensic evidence. Lord Allard was a self-made multi-millionaire and was the founder and managing director of Cranberry Crunch. In a statement released today, the Metropolitan Police have said that the investigation is ongoing and will broaden its scope of inquiry and will now involve the Specialist Operations unit of Scotland Yard.

'The Irish Prime Minister Dr Garret Fitzgerald has called for greater co-operation in combatting terrorism in the wake of the Harrods bombing. Writing in today's Times, he says, "This is a moment of emotional solidarity across the Irish Sea." And goes on, "It is the duty of leadership to ensure that enduring good comes out of these tragedies."

'This is Philip Hyman for BBC News.'

'Thank you Philip. Now, as promised we have Mr James Prior, Secretary of State for Northern Ireland in our radio car... Mr Prior, can you hear me?...'

Angus turned off the radio. 'Bloody hell. A Specialist Operations unit... This thing is getting bigger by the minute... Who'd have thought it possible, eh? And we thought that old Digby was the culprit.'

'We weren't alone though, were we? The police had their suspicions too,' added Sam.

'What I want to know is why anyone would want Allard dead in the first place,' wondered Brian.

'Beats me... And it was bloody irresponsible of them to use my MontBlanc... They could have used their own bleeding pen!'

'Did the police never return it?' asked Brian.

'No... well, it's a murder weapon... Don't think you usually get given those back.' Angus started the ignition and they continued on their way.

Sam looked at Angus. 'Feels a bit strange going down there for a second time, don't you think?'

Angus shrugged. Sam looked in the mirror at Brian in the back. 'Don't you think so, Brian?'

'I know what you mean... Having spied on him first time round and pretended that we didn't know that the police were questioning him, I do feel a bit of a fraud. But some people think that what Angus and I do for a living is a bit of a fraud... You know, the black arts... Selling people complete crap that they don't need.'

'That's complete bloody bollocks,' retorted Angus. 'The people who suffer the most are the poor sods like us who create the ads.'

'Hang on a bit. How can you say that, Angus?' demanded Sam.

'Let me explain... I had this very conversation with Magnus last week in the pub, and he reckons that any good copywriter or art director worth his salt will believe passionately in the products they are working on, to the point that they actually end up buying these products for themselves. And he reckons that he's possessed more crap cars, crap investments, crap boilers, crap holidays and crap cameras as a result of being fooled by his own compelling copy.'

Sam laughed out loud. 'That's hilarious.'

'Don't tell Magnus that... I think he was being quite serious... Mind you, I think we were both a bit pissed at the time.'

———— ··●·· ————

They were doing pretty well for time. Hugh had invited them for lunch at one o'clock and it was only 12.15 and they were now really close, so when Angus spotted a very pretty thatched pub, he instinctively pulled into the car park.

'What do you reckon? Quick one for the road, or at least the rest of the road?'

Brian grinned. 'Would be silly not to, I suppose.'

The barman was a jovial ruddy-faced man with a South London accent, and within minutes the four of them were deep in conversation. It turned out that Colin the barman had been an art director at Saatchi and Saatchi for some years and jacked it all in to run the pub.

'Thing about the industry is that it's really going downhill... It was one of the reasons I got out when I did,' explained Colin. 'I mean there are so few good commercials on the box these days - with the exception of that brilliant campaign for real fires, of course... That one is so good.'

'Yeah it's not bad,' agreed Angus.

'Not bad? Are you kidding? It's probably the best TV campaign that's graced our screens for at least ten years... Apparently, it was created by some junior team...'

'Is that right?' chipped in Brian.

'Yeah... I don't know how they got Brian Clough and Don Revie to interact in the way they did. It's a thing of beauty and so funny... How about you guys? Have you done anything I'd have seen?'

Brian shrugged. 'Nah... We just get to shovel the shit.'

'Yeah. We get all the DM crap and shelf-wobblers to do.'

'Shelf wobblers? Oh no, you poor sods. Let me get you another round. This one's on me as a form of commiseration.'

Samantha had to excuse herself to go to the bathroom, and once through the door, she broke into a fit of giggles. Those boys were funny, and it had been such a long time since she'd been able to laugh this much.

CHAPTER TWENTY-NINE

'Hello, Mark Hammond speaking. Yes, this is the Specialist Operations Unit, Scotland Yard. How can I help?'

There was a long pause as Mark Hammond listened carefully to the man with a very distinctive Italian accent. The call lasted no more than a couple of minutes, and the caller had an impeccable grasp of English.

'Thank you very much indeed for your call, Mr Rossi. I will pass on this information immediately. Thank you.'

He put down the phone and closed his eyes momentarily. Then he lifted the receiver and dialled.

'Hello, Sir. I've just had a call from our counterparts in Milan... They want to draw our attention to Alitalia flight 830 from Milan to Heathrow. A Mr Antonio Brambilla is on that flight with two accomplices. They are known to the authorities and are being monitored. Brambilla is the son of Luca Brambilla and is very dangerous. And to complicate matters, there are two retired members of the Antimafia Commission on the same flight tracking them: a Mr Giuseppe Esposito and a Giovanni Accardo. They are all likely to be armed... According to Rossi, Esposito is a bit of a loose cannon. He was forced out of the Commission two years ago for overstepping the mark... No Sir, the nature of Brambilla's trip is unknown...Yes Sir... Of course, I'll get onto them right away.'

CHAPTER THIRTY

———— · · ● · · ————

Angus parked outside the house. In the sunshine, the house looked prettier than he remembered.

'I wonder if wild boar is on the menu,' pondered Brian.

'You know, for someone of the Jewish faith, you seem unhealthily obsessed with non-kosher fare,' said Sam.

'Ah, that's because I'm not a Jew. I'm just Jew-ish... Not the whole hog.'

Angus chuckled. 'Very good Finklebrain. I don't suppose any of us could manage a whole hog - maybe half a hog,' He pressed the doorbell. There was no sign of life, so he then decided to use the door knocker in case the bell wasn't working, and in doing so the front door opened slightly. It hadn't been properly closed.

They all looked at each other. 'Should we go inside?' ventured Sam.

Angus nodded. 'I reckon so...' He stepped into the hallway and raised his voice. 'Hello, Hugh. We've arrived.' There was no response. It was an elegant house with an abundance of antique furniture. The dining room table had already been set for lunch and a grandfather clock in the hall just chimed on the half-hour. A Siamese cat appeared from behind a sofa and rubbed against Samantha's leg. 'Hello, sweetie.' Sam bent down and stroked the cat who now purred.

They moved together methodically into the kitchen. A piece of toast had popped up in the toaster and a mug of tea sat on the granite work surface.

While Sam and Angus nosed around the kitchen, Brian let himself into a room adjacent to the kitchen.

'Shit! Fuck!'

Sam and Angus looked round. Brian was standing in the doorway looking very pale. 'I think I'm going to be sick.' And then he was.

———— ··•·· ————

The body was slumped in an armchair. There was a large bloodstain on his torso and his neck had been cut. Angus blocked the doorway. 'You don't want to go in there, Sam. It's not good.' He put his arm around her. She was shivering from shock.

Brian was rinsing his mouth with water. 'We're going to have to go straight to the police.'

Angus agreed. 'Yeah. Let's get out of here, and don't for fuck's sake touch anything. This is a crime scene.'

In the hall, they were confronted by three large figures. Antonio pointed a gun at Angus.

'You are not going anywhere.' Antonio turned to his associates. 'Legali e mettili in macchina.' The two others swiftly tied each of their hands behind their backs.

'What are you going to do with us?' asked Sam nervously.

'You are going to come on a little drive with us.'

198

CHAPTER THIRTY-ONE

— · • ● • · —

'Gentlemen, I thank you sincerely from the bottom of my heart for taking the time to come here today. I can assure you that it will be well worth your time.'

Luca Brambilla dimmed the lights and pressed a button on his remote control, which brought a large screen down from the ceiling. The ten suited men around the table were clearly from a diverse range of countries, but they all spoke English, and Luca seemed to know them all.

'Until now gentlemen, the family has been able to deliver a highly competitive return on your initial investment. Any investment as you know will balance risk with reward. And if I'm honest, the level of risk that you have been prepared to shoulder has been relatively high. What I am proposing today is to lower that risk considerably. But not, I might add, at the cost of your profit. Far from it. Our new business model will in fact be helping you to enhance the return on your investment. Let me explain...' He clicked his remote control and brought up the first slide. 'The family's first foray into the food industry was by chance three years ago when we helped out an old family friend with his struggling restaurant business in Florence. This was the balance sheet before we stepped in.' He clicked the remote control. 'And this was the balance sheet for the business three years later. We were able to curb the overheads, stifle competition, and increase profit margins; while also syphoning many of our liquid assets through this legitimate business… It was, in short, an eye-opening exercise for us, and one we are now replicating on a much larger scale. To date, we have invested in over 250 restaurants. And by next year this figure will double.' He brought up another slide. 'We have also identified huge profit opportunities in farmland leasing thanks to the European Economic Community's farming subsidies. By simply leasing swathes of cheap public land, we can claim significant sums in farming subsidies from the EEC. The profit margins as you can see here are eye-watering: 1,000 hectares of land would qualify for 20 billion Lira a year in EEC subsidies for a leasing outlay of just 1 billion Lira. That, gentlemen, represents a 2,000 per cent profit margin.

'Our third strand of revenue will come from food production. To utilise much of our farmland, which is of fairly low quality, we propose to corner the market in wild boar production and supply. Wild boar is a premium meat product with huge potential across Europe and further afield. Indeed, we have reason to believe that its popularity will grow in Europe exponentially over the next few years. By simply making our presence felt and removing any competition, we aim to establish ourselves as the largest supplier of wild boar in Europe - putting us in a position to control prices and enjoy very healthy returns.

'These three revenue streams are the basis for our new business model. A model that is already reaping rewards. We have prepared detailed projections based on these three revenue strands. Please do take as many copies of these documents as you require. Should you have any further questions over the next few days, please feel free to contact me directly through the usual channel. And that, gentlemen, concludes my short but hopefully insightful presentation.'

CHAPTER THIRTY-TWO

'It looks like he was murdered very recently, Sarge.' It wasn't the first time Officer Stephen Hobson had seen a dead body. It was something of an occupational hazard when you worked with Special Operations. It didn't really affect him like it affected others, and he had certainly never puked as some did.

'Yeah... You're not wrong there, officer. Let's get forensics down and seal it all off.' Sergeant Charles Garrett had seen it all. Nothing phased him. He switched on his radio, which was low on battery, so he returned to the car and unhooked the radio and called in. 'Sir, we've found a body at the property. IC1, male, mid-60s... He's been shot in the stomach and has been stabbed in the neck... The area is being sealed and forensics are on the case... Yes, Sir. Of course...

They had arrived at the agreed location ten minutes early. Nothing was going to plan. And he had three bloody hostages to deal with. It was out of character for Antonio to mess up this badly.

They pulled into the side of the road. There were a couple of detached houses overlooking the playing field. One looked particularly unkempt and had a handrail up to the front door and an attached garage. Antonio pointed to the house. There was no way they could sit here in broad daylight

'Non possiamo restare qui. È troppo pericoloso. Proviamo questa casa.' The two Italian sidekicks jumped out of the car, made their way over to the house, and knocked at the door. As soon as the elderly occupant answered in his slippers, the two men had bundled him inside at gunpoint. Within seconds one of the Italians reappeared and opened up the garage. Antonio looked in the mirror. The three hostages were behaving themselves. He started up the engine and drove the car straight into the garage and turned off the ignition. He got out and opened the back door.

'You three get out now.' He led all three of them towards the house.

Brian should have been feeling terrified. But strangely, he wasn't. He was more mystified than anything else. Who were these Italian fuckers and why had they murdered Digby? Then for some inexplicable reason, he started to think about his parents. What would his father have said in the circumstances? What would his advice to his son have been? *Brian, whatever you do, don't make matters worse, son. When you get inside the house, be helpful. Be a mensch... Offer them all tea.*

He smiled to himself as he followed Angus and Sam towards the house.

Angus was feeling terrified, not about himself but for Sam. He didn't know who the hell they were and he didn't particularly care. They could do what the fuck they liked. He just prayed that they wouldn't hurt the girl he loved. And he loved her more intensely now than ever before.

<hr/>

Sam was terrified. This whole thing was her worst possible nightmare. She wanted to wake up and be free from this hell. Numb with fear, she couldn't think straight. All she could feel was Angus's stubble on her ear and wet tears rolling down her face. She hadn't even realised she was crying.

<hr/>

As Antonio led them towards the house, there was a sudden succession of gunshots coming from the other side of the road. Angus instinctively pushed Sam to the ground and Brian acted similarly.

Antonio had been knocked to the floor but didn't seem to have been injured. It was fortunate that he had been wearing his bullet-proof vest. Now he returned fire while lying prostrate on the ground. And the two Italians were also returning fire from the sitting room window.

Brian gestured with the movement of his head to a nearby garden wall no more than a couple of feet high, and all three of them made a dash for it and threw themselves behind it.

They were out of harm's way for the moment at least.

CHAPTER THIRTY-THREE

'Hello. You are through to Emergency Services. Which service do you require?'

'All bloody three of 'em… And fast… All hell's broken out next door. I tell you it's like World War bloody three here… Haven't got a fucking clue what's goin' on… They're bloody pensioners in their eighties for Christ's sake… And I don't think they're having an indoor fireworks party…'

CHAPTER THIRTY-FOUR

Giuseppe was a wily fox. He had caught Antonio by surprise thanks to a nifty bit of discreet phone tapping at the hotel where the Italians had stayed. It's remarkable what a little bit of technical know-how and good old-fashioned bribery could achieve.

Giuseppe, Giovanni and his five sons only had handguns but there were seven of them against three, and the seven of them would certainly have had more ammunition. It was only a matter of time before they'd nail the bastards.

The only thing that worried Giuseppe was the possibility that this location was some kind of rendezvous - but with whom, Giuseppe had no idea.

As the gunfire intensified, the answer to Giuseppe's quandary gradually became apparent. The hum of a distant engine slowly grew closer and closer until the sound became deafening and a helicopter swooped down and hovered in range of the house. As it did, there was a prolonged burst of machine gun fire from the heavens, and Antonio and his two accomplices ran from the house towards the playing field.

Try as they might, there was no way Giuseppe and his men could break cover to take potshots without being killed. And by the time the machine gun stopped, the three thugs had made their connection and were in the air.

Angus had managed to untie his hands and was now untying Sam's. As soon as he had, she clung to him eagerly like a limpet, and he kissed the top of her head.

'Excuse me... Sorry for butting in and all that, but I don't suppose you could untie your art director while you're at it could you?'

Angus and Sam looked over at Brian and in no time at all, all three of them were laughing uncontrollably.

Sergeant Garrett got out of his car and walked towards the house while talking into his radio.

One of Giovanni's sons was having his arm bandaged by a neighbour who was a paramedic, and there were two old boys jabbering away in a mixture of Italian and English.

'Excuse me, gentlemen... I assume I am addressing Giuseppe Esposito and Giovanni Accardo.'

The two men looked up. 'Si signore... Yes Sir.' Giuseppe extended his right hand and Sergeant Garrett shook it.

'I am Sergeant Garrett from Special Operations.'

'Very nice to make your acquaintance, Sergeant Garrett. This is my friend Giovanni Accardo.'

Giovanni shook the sergeant's hand and smiled broadly. 'How may we help you?'

'If you could accompany me into the house, I'd like to take statements from you and everyone else.'

———— ··•·· ————

Antonio had been shaken. It was the first time his operation hadn't run smoothly. More disturbingly, he simply didn't know who was behind the attack. They had had plenty of enemies from rival families in the past, but that was in the past. They'd settled their differences, and had let bygones be bygones for almost ten years now. It could only have been that prick Giuseppe who should by all rights be dead anyway.

The helicopter banked hard to the right as Antonio pulled off his bullet-proof vest. Shit! He'd taken four direct hits. He was lucky to be alive.

They were making good progress now.

If it had been Giuseppe behind the attack, he had clearly been supported by others. There must have been at least five of them if not more.

He put his hand on the pilot's shoulder. 'Quanto tempo ci vorrà?'

'15 minuti - massimo.'

'Perfect.' He was anxious to be well away from this godforsaken island. The English police would soon be on his heels. This whole operation had been cursed from the off. He could only relax when he was back on Italian soil, and with that thought in his head, he pulled his vest back on. He wasn't going to take any chances.

The swathe of green beyond the grey tarmac and red brick came into view and the helicopter began to lose height. They were just above the tree line now as they banked hard to the right one final time. Antonio could see the little white planes parked neatly in their allotted spaces. Marco was a skilled pilot. He was the best. With a gentle bump, they were now down. The familiar sleek lines of the family's Cessna Citation came into view. It was a reassuring sight. The rotor blades had ceased spinning and Marco gave them the thumbs up and slid open the canopy. Antonio couldn't get off quickly enough, and was followed by the other two. They raced up the steps and Antonio headed straight for the cabin while the other two sat by the open door where they observed the ground crew wheeling away the steps. Antonio stuck his head into the pilot's cabin.

'We're all here. Do we have clearance yet?'

The pilot turned in his seat. 'We do and are third in line for the runway.'

'Grazie al diavolo.'

Antonio sank into the leather seat and closed his eyes. He could feel the aircraft moving slowly now towards the runway. He could have been killed; he could have been arrested; it had been a messy operation; but he had no real grounds for being unhappy; the mission had been accomplished; and he was about to get away with murder. Yet again.

CHAPTER THIRTY-FIVE

'So you and your friend here are, or were, I should say, members of the Antimafia Commission.'

Giuseppe nodded. 'That is correct, signore.'

'And you also say that the man you were following is named Antonio Brambilla.'

'Si Signore. That is correct. He is a very dangerous man who only days ago tried to kill me.'

'And you say that this Antonio Brambilla has form.'

'Form? I am sorry. Which form would this be?'

'No... Not form like paperwork. What I mean is that this Antonio Brambilla has a history of violence.'

'Oh yes... He most certainly has murdered many people in Italy... But he is clever... He never leaves any, how you say, incriminatory evidence behind. So we can never prove that he was responsible.'

'And do you have any idea why he might be in the UK?'

'I have no idea why he would be here, but I would guess that he was here to murder someone.'

'Why should he want to do that?'

Guiseppe shrugged. 'How long is a piece of string?... I have no idea... But this family usually murders for one thing only - business. If you get in their way, they'll remove you... That's why they tried to kill me... I am trying to change the law to make it more difficult to lease land in Italy and claim EEC subsidies. They don't like me for doing this because it will stop them earning billions of Lira from their land leasing programme.'

Sergeant Garrett was taking this all down in his notebook.

'This is very interesting, Mr Esposito... A murder was committed not very far from here...'

'Excuse me?... And had the murder victim been shot in the stomach and stabbed in the neck, Sergeant?'

'My God!... How on earth did you know that?'

'This is the signature of Antonio Brambilla... Always a cut to the neck with a different blade every time and a gunshot to the stomach - always with a different gun.'

As Sergeant Garrett scribbled in his notebook, there was a knock at the door, and the elderly and bewildered-looking owner answered in his slippers.

'Hello. I'm Inspector Bicknell... I understand that there has been something tantamount to World War II breaking out here.'

The old boy was looking very confused. 'I thought the war was over in 1945, Inspector.'

'Yes Sir... I mean it as a figure of speech.'

The old man nodded. 'Terrible thing war, you know... Served in the British 8th Army, inspector... Saw action in Tripoli... When we ran out of ammunition, we killed men with our bare hands... Terrible thing war, Inspector... Would you like a nice cup of tea? We have Hobnobs by the way... They are very good for dunking, I find... Do you like Hobnobs, Inspector?'

214

'Well, I um... I er... just need to...'

'Yes, of course, you can use the little boy's room... It's upstairs. It's first on the right. You need to pull the chain quite hard, Inspector. Doesn't always work first time... The wife has a thing about us blokes peeing on the floor... So please do be a little bit careful, otherwise it's me who gets the blame.'

'Excellent... Shall I come in then?... I'd just like to ask you some questions.'

The old man looked a little worried. 'Not too hot at answering questions. Don't normally get very many right. Mind you, I did get five correct on University Challenge once... Nice man that Bamber Gasgoine.... Strange name though, don't you think?... I mean, why would any parent call their son Bamber, particularly when it's followed by Gasgoine? It's a bit cruel don't you think?'

'I hadn't really thought about it...'

'One of your colleagues is already here, Inspector. He's asking questions too... Why don't you come in? We can have a bit of a quiz.'

'Thank you...' Inspector Bicknell stepped into the hallway and was led to the kitchen where he saw Sergeant Garrett at the table with Giuseppe. 'Good afternoon, Sergeant. I am Inspector Bicknell.'

Sergeant Garrett rose to his feet. 'Ah, Inspector. I am Sergeant Garrett from Special Operations. We were tipped off about a Mr Antonio Brambilla entering the country, and it looks as if he may very well be the man behind two murders including the infamous Lord Allard murder. I am interviewing Mr Esposito here who used to be a member of the Antimafia Commission. And we are trying to establish a possible motive... Was there anything that both Lord Allard and this last victim, Digby, had in common, Inspector?'

'Yes, Sergeant... Pigs.'

'I beg your pardon?'

'Pigs... Well, more accurately, wild boar.'

CHAPTER THIRTY-SIX

———— ·•●•· ————

'He's ever so nice, you know. Did you have a meeting with him before?'

Angus smiled politely. He was a little bit nervous. He'd never been on live television before. 'We had a little chat earlier with him. He seems really nice... Very down to earth.'

'Oh, he is. Everyone loves Russell. He's an absolute sweetie. He used to teach, you know.'

'Oh, did he? I didn't know that...'

'But there's no need to get anxious. Just be yourself. He's always so good with his guests. And I'll tell you something else... He thinks the world of his mum... We met her last week, you know... Lovely lady... So proud of her son... Well, you would be, wouldn't you?'

Annie was applying makeup to Angus and having sips of tea between brushstrokes. Sam was next to him having her hair seen to by a June who was very quiet, and Brian was on the far side being looked after by Linda, the most glamorous of the threesome.

'Your mum must be very proud of you... I mean, you three haven't been out of the papers for weeks, have you?'

'No, I suppose we have had a fair bit of publicity... I'm not sure that my mother would be so impressed, though. She probably thinks it's all a bit tacky, to be honest. Not too sure that she really approves of me being in the advertising industry. She was hoping I'd have a career at the Foreign Office.'

'Oh, dear... She's a bit out of touch, isn't she? You don't want to go and work for that lot. They're all a lot of stuffed shirts. The advertising business is far more exciting... I mean, you get to meet such interesting people... like me.' At this point, she laughed like a drain. 'I'm joking, of course... And besides, the money in advertising is really good, too... I'm sure you are doing very nicely for yourself...'

Angus blushed a little. 'Yeah... We are looked after very well... We're lucky I suppose. We have a terrific boss.'

She put down her blusher. 'You're not lucky, luv. You're talented. Those commercials for real fires... They are the best flipping things on the telly. I nearly wet myself when I saw that one with Dr Who and the Dalek... I don't know how you come up with them... So don't you give me that stuff about being lucky. You deserve your success. You are bloody talented.'

Angus blushed again. It was the first time anyone had been so effusive about the work he and Brian had produced. It was crazy really. At the end of the day, they were just 40-second bits of film. They weren't novels or feature films. But it was nice to be appreciated like this by a complete stranger.

———— ·•●•· ————

'You've got lovely hair.'

'Have I?'

'Yeah - it's naturally wavy. I know girls who'd die for hair like that.' Linda applied some smelly spray and combed it through Brian's locks. 'Talking of dying, those murders were all very peculiar weren't they?'

'You can say that again. Sometimes I wake up in the morning thinking the whole thing has been a bad dream.'

'And being kidnapped... I mean, that must have been terrifying beyond words.'

'Yes... I wouldn't recommend it.'

She laughed. He was nice... She'd seen them all doing this job. Half of them were ok. Half were arrogant shits. A handful were really nice. Russell Harty, of course, was one of her favourites. He'd always find time to chat to them and had been known to buy them little presents. 'So where do you live, Brian?'

'I have a little flat in Hampstead, but when I say little I mean really minuscule. About enough space to swing an ant.'

She laughed again. She had a lovely smile. 'Hampstead is dead posh though... Doesn't that Peter Cook live in Hampstead?'

'Yeah... He lives down the road to me... I helped him to his door a while back. He'd had a few I think.'

'You are joking...'

'No... Why?'

'You are not going to believe this... But I did his makeup last week... I was a bit nervous because he's one of my heroes... Anyway, he was chatting away and being really friendly. And then he asked me what I thought of people in the showbiz world, and I said you know, it was like society in general - there was good and bad... He said I was being very diplomatic.

And then he said that his whole perception of the human race had gone up inestimably since he was helped to his front door by a young man - a complete stranger. He said he was charming and he felt so bad because he didn't even have the decency to thank him or ask him what his name was.'

'Blimey... Are you being serious? Really?'

'Of course... Honest to God... And it was you... That's incredible.'

'That is incredible. I can hardly believe he said that... You've made my day. Thank you.'

'It's my pleasure.'

'I don't suppose you like jazz, do you, Linda?'

'I love jazz.'

'Do you fancy coming to Ronnie Scotts tonight? Oscar Peterson is playing and I've just been offered a couple of tickets.'

'I'd love to Brian. Thank you. Oscar Peterson is a genius. That's so kind of you.'

'It's my pleasure, Linda.'

———— ··•●•·· ————

The titles were rolling and then the band started to play the theme tune and the live audience showed its appreciation by applauding enthusiastically, and the producer of the show gave him the signal and queued him in.

'Ladies and Gents, we have a wonderful line-up for your entertainment tonight. We have this year's winner of the Edinburgh Festival Perrier Award - Walter Zerlin Junior whose farce *Running Around the Stage Like a Lunatic* features 17 parts all played miraculously by Walter Zerlin himself who, by the way, is a barrister during the day. We also have the inimitable and hugely talented Gnaff Ensemble who are going to give us a sneak preview of their Christmas punk number, *Free Kings*. But before welcoming them onto the show, we have three young people who have become national celebrities. They've been all over the news having been mixed up in the dreadful and totally surreal murder cases of Lord Allard and Hugh Digby, and were, of course, kidnapped by the suspected murderer who is, I might add, still at large. Ladies and gentlemen, will you please put your hands together and welcome Brian Finkle, Angus Lovejoy and Samantha Pilkington.'

CHAPTER THIRTY-SEVEN

L'Arcangelo was one of the finest restaurants in Naples with one of the best views of the majestic sweep of Naples harbour. On warm days like today, a table on the terrace beneath the pergola supporting the climbing vines was the closest you could get to heaven on earth.

As the little white boats bobbed and twinkled like diamonds in the sunlight on the deep cobalt waves, the waiter placed the menus on the table with a basket of freshly baked ciabatta and olive oil. An elegant woman in white studied the menu. The man seated next to her was balding and sported spectacles. His name was Bettino Craxi. He was Italy's new Prime Minister.

'I can certainly recommend today's special.'

The woman smiled. 'And what may that be?'

'Tuscan wild boar ragu with pappardelle pasta.'

'Sounds delicious. I'll have that please.'

Bettino Craxi smiled at the waiter. 'E lo stesso per me per favore.'

The waiter bowed. 'Grazie. Ottima scelta.'

CHAPTER THIRTY-EIGHT

'Hello. This is Mario Gripaldo speaking... Yes, this is Harrods, London.'

There was a long pause.

'As it happens, we would be very interested in stocking wild boar in our food hall as our current supplier has been unable to meet our requirements due to unforeseen circumstances... No, we haven't any other arrangements in place...

'How extraordinary, I too come from Siena... It is indeed a small world... I would be very happy to try your samples. I could do tomorrow afternoon at 3.00 if that suits you...

'Grazie mille. Non vedo l'ora di vedervi.'

CHAPTER THIRTY-NINE

Magnus was deep in thought with his feet on the desk. He had his best ideas when he was in this very position. A bottle of Stella Artois tended to help matters.

The tap on his door interrupted his train of thought.

'Come in if you must...'

Kenneth entered looking a little sheepish. 'Sorry guv'nor. I didn't want to interrupt the creative flow.'

'That's alright. We've got a pair of creative geniuses down the corridor. So if you've just gone and stifled my next award-winning campaign, we'll just wheel the boys in.'

'Fair enough.'

'Actually, that reminds me, Ken. We need to talk about Brian and Angus. I'm hearing on the grapevine that they're being approached by rival agencies... I really don't want to lose them. I know it's not what we had planned but I'd like to offer them a bonus.'

Kenneth nodded. 'Ok. Let me talk to Paul... I agree with you. We need to hang on to them... I'll get back to you before the end of play. I'm sure we can put something together.'

'Great... Thanks, Kenneth. I appreciate that... Now, what can I do you for?'

'I have just come off the phone to Tarquin Allard... Do you want the good news or the bad news first?'

'Oh, shit sticks... Give me the good news first, Ken.'

'Well, the good news is that Tarquin has confirmed officially that there will be no review process for Cranberry Crunch and that the little toerag Ogden Baggott has been told to basically shove his design guidelines where the sun don't shine. In addition, sales of Cranberry Crunch have risen very dramatically in the last month due to the extraordinary publicity of Lord Allard's murder. In short, the client is a very happy bunny.'

'Wow, that's a result.'

'Yes and no.'

'I knew you were going to say that. Hit me with the shit.'

'Well, the shit as you so delicately put it is that sales of Cranberry Crunch have been so fucking spectacular that they can't make the stuff quickly enough... They simply can't cope... So they want to cut all marketing activity.'

'All marketing activity?'

'Yep... Afraid so... Not as much as a shelf wobbler.'

'Oh fuck.'

'Oh fuck, indeed.'

CHAPTER FORTY

'Hello Brian, it's mum here. How are you darling?... I'm just phoning because dad and I just saw you on the Russell Harty Show... You were marvellous... We are so proud of you... Listen, I'm going to put dad on the line. He wants to say hello...'

'Hello Brian, it's dad. Your mother and I enjoyed that show. We were kvelling. It was wonderful. And you know that Walter Zerlin fellow who was on before you... His father is a member of our synagogue... It's a small world, isn't it?...

'That's fantastic Brian... Susan, they've given him another bonus... And you would like to take us where? Well, that would be lovely, Brian... Susan, he wants to take us to the Ritz for lunch... And you want to introduce us to who? Susan, he wants to introduce us to a girl... I'm putting mum back on... She's taken the receiver.'

'You've met a nice girl, Brian? Mazel tov. That's lovely... Of course, we want to meet her. Tell me, is she a nice Jewish girl?... She's a nice girl but you don't know about the Jewish bit yet... So what's her name?... Maurice, her name is Linda Green... Well, Green could be a Jewish name...You can live in hope...'

CHAPTER FORTY-ONE

It was a strange pre-fab-looking building on the outskirts of Debden in Essex that overlooked a disused gravel pit and an uninspiring council estate that was well past its use-by date. Kenneth parked his Saab in one of a handful of spaces on the forecourt and switched off the engine.

His heart sank. 'Well, it's not exactly Blenheim Palace, is it?'

'Oh, I don't know... If you were from the slums of Mombasa, this place would look like Nirvana.'

'That's what I love about you, Bernard. Always the optimist... What about you Magnus?... You've been uncharacteristically quiet in the back.'

'Sorry, Ken. I've been a bit distracted by this Magimix brief... I think I have an idea that's a bit... well, Shakespearean in concept.'

'Good heavens, Commander... Sounds like you've got a bard-on.'

'Very good, Bernard... Well, to be honest, Kenneth, I wasn't as enthusiastic about it as you were... But then again, your reasoning about their connection with the Home Office was what won me over. And you can't deny that this bloke has impressive connections; and as you always say, it's the connections that count.'

Kenneth nodded and opened the door. 'Oh well. Let's see what he has to offer.'

A young girl in a fluffy pink jumper and dayglow pink nail varnish let them in. 'Good afternoon. Welcome to Beta Recording Systems. Is Adrian expecting you?'

'Yes. It's Kenneth Drayton, Magnus O'Shea and Bernard Hamilton. We had an appointment to see him at 2 o'clock.'

She checked her diary. 'Oh yes, silly of me. I had the wrong month open, and it's my wrong time of the month, too - not that you need to know that... Why don't you take a seat? I'll tell Adrian you're here... I'm afraid the coffee machine is out of order, but to be honest that's probably a blessing in disguise. I've been trying to persuade Adrian to change it before we poison someone. But do help yourself to water.' She picked up the phone. 'Adrian, you have a Mr Draycot, O'Shea and Hamlyn to see you... okey dokey... Would you like to go through?... It's the last door on the left, opposite the Gents.'

Kenneth smiled and they all got to their feet.

'Ah, Kenneth. Thank you so much for taking time out to traipse over to this backwater.'

'Not at all. Thank you for inviting us.' He shook Adrian warmly by the hand. 'This is our creative director Magnus O'Shea, and our senior account director Bernard Hamilton.'

Adrian shook their hands and gestured to a tired-looking sofa by the wall that sat below a large map of the world with a profusion of red pins protruding from its surface.

'Well, first of all, I'd like to share some very good news with you. I have spoken to the Home Office this morning and they are very happy with the way our machines have performed, and will be adopting them as part of the proposed Police and Criminal Evidence Act, which they expect to come into force sometime next year.'

Kenneth nodded and smiled. 'That is very good news, Adrian. Many congratulations.'

'Thank you... So, this is where you chaps come in... As I see it, there are two potential markets for our machines. Firstly, we have the world's police forces. And in this respect, I am already talking to South Korea, Belize, Toga, and Bahrain through interpreters.

'And secondly, there is the domestic market. And here we're talking about families with young children who they want to protect from hearing inappropriate material like, for example, the Derek and Clive Live recordings.'

'Oh yes...', said Bernard, 'I remember those well. They were very naughty... Completely inappropriate for children though...'

'As you know our machines are tamper-proof and lockable. So no young child will be able to operate the machine once it has been locked. And we could patent this as a unique 'child lock'. It could be like a safety belt for cassette players.'

'I see what you mean,' said Magnus. 'A kind of *Clunk Click Every Track* campaign.'

'Oooh. That's very clever... I do like that.'

'And in terms of media and budget, what exactly did you have in mind, Adrian?' asked Kenneth.

'Well, initially what I would require from you would be literature and educational films to sell the concept to our two target markets. And once we had some clients on board, we'd be in a position to invest in producing a Direct Mail campaign in the various markets to our two target audiences.

'So in answer to your question about the budget, the initial spend will be very small. Somewhere in the region of 5 to 10K for the information pieces. But a DM campaign rolled out to different markets could be pretty big - possibly 100K if not more - depending of course on the take-up.'

'That sounds very interesting, ' said Kenneth as he gave Magnus one of his surreptitious looks. 'Could I just stop you there? I'm afraid I need the little boy's room.'

'Yes, of course. You don't have far to go. It's just outside.'

'Actually, I will do likewise... Bit of a weak bladder, I'm afraid,' added Magnus.

Once inside the Gents, they spoke in hushed voices.

'I'm sorry mate, you were right from the outset... The man's nuts.'

'It's alright Ken... You never can tell until you see the whites of their eyes so to speak. But I agree with you. I mean, South Korea, Belize, Toga, and Bahrain. It's bonkers... And these machines will be tomorrow's chip paper before you can say, Christopher Robin.'

'So how are we going to play this?... I don't want to give the man any false hopes. But by the same token, I don't want to hurt his feelings... Never a good ploy. He might end up as Marketing Director of Barclays Bank next year.'

'Leave it with me, Ken... I have an idea that will work a treat.'

'That's what I love about you creative bods - you've always got an idea up your sleeve. I'm going to keep schtum then.'

They both returned to Adrian's office and took their seats.

'Well, gentlemen, that sort of sums up where I am and what I'd like you to do to help... What do you reckon?'

 'First of all Adrian, I'd like to thank you for talking us through this... It is a very interesting project. But I'm going to take a back seat and let

Magnus give you his opinion. When it comes to creative work, Magnus always has the last word in these matters.'

'Thanks, Ken. Now Adrian. I'm going to be very honest with you here... I don't think we as an advertising agency have the very specialist skills you require to bring this exceptional machine to market... You see, we are very good at creating imaginative advertising campaigns. But you don't require that... You need a good, solid, effective information campaign. That's not what we do.

'Now, we could go away and create what you ask us to, but if I am honest, there are other companies out there who specialise in this kind of work who will undoubtedly do a far better job than us, and their fees may very well be lower than ours.'

Adrian's face dropped. He was clearly disappointed.

'But there is good news, Adrian. Because there is in fact a perfect solution that we as an agency can full-heartedly endorse here and now. And our advice won't cost you a penny.'

Magnus had Adrian eating out of his hand. He was all ears.

CHAPTER FORTY-TWO

'Hello. Is that Mr Ogden Baggott speaking?... Ah, excellent. Let me introduce myself. My name is Adrian Vickery, and I am the founder and Managing Director of Beta Recording Systems. I have been recommended your design service by Mr Magnus O'Shea from Gordon Deedes Rutter. Mr O'Shea holds you in very high regard. I have a proposition that may be of interest to you...'

EPILOGUE

Paddy O'Leary and Sean Flaherty, the two tramps who had installed themselves outside the offices of RHB, were now singing an extremely rude ditty, the words of which cannot possibly be repeated here. They may have been blissfully happy, but the creative director of said agency, a certain Tom Haggard was not in the least bit happy. He had an important fashion house client arriving for a presentation in half an hour, and the last thing he wanted was this sophisticated Italian client to be greeted by an inebriated couple of vagrants serenading him with filthy obscenities that left little to the imagination.

He took the lift down to reception and let himself out of the front doors.

Paddy stopped singing and raised his beer can to Tom.

Tom forced a smile and tried not to breathe in. 'I say chaps. You seem in fine fettle this morning. Always nice to hear such good, strong voices. And I'm always up for a good sing-song myself. But I take the view that such melodious delights should really be shared fairly... So here's what I'm going to do...' He reached into his jacket pocket and withdrew a wallet from which he pulled eight crisp fifty-pound notes. 'By way of a thank you, I'd like to offer you £200 each, on the condition that you pick yourselves up and sit on the doorstep of the building at the end of the road. It has a sign outside that reads Gordon Deedes Rutter. You can't miss it. I think it only fair that they, too, can enjoy your rendition.' He handed them each the money.

Paddy belched and just stared at the four Banknotes in his hand with Sir Christopher Wren staring back at him in his very fancy wig and fine silk attire. He'd never even seen a 50-pound note before - let alone four of the buggers. He gave Tom a military salute and dragged his mate up by the collar. And the two of them swayed and staggered down the road to their new home.

Half an hour later a large black Daimler arrived and parked on the Corner of Great Pulteney Street. A dapper chauffeur emerged from the driver's side and opened the back door and an elegant grey-haired man accompanied by two blonde models got out and entered the offices of RHB.

The number plate on the Daimler was particularly distinctive. It read BRAM1.

ACKNOWLEDGEMENTS

Thanks go in large part to my brother David. It was his idea that I should write a comic murder mystery set in the advertising world of the 1980s since it was a world I knew well and wouldn't have to spend endless hours researching. Whilst I had half the book vaguely sketched out in my head, the second and crucial part of the book was proving difficult to resolve - until David and I had lengthy discussions about the plot over the phone. As a result, we were able to hit on an idea that seemed to work pretty well. And to give this idea credence and backbone, David unearthed a brilliantly researched and fascinating article written for the Financial Times by Hannah Roberts in 2018. This was not only important in adding grist to the mill and making the plot credible; it also gave the book another dynamic dimension and physical location. Thanks also go to Andrew Glennie for taking the time to check my use of the Italian language. Lastly and by no means least, I'd like to thank my wife Jennifer and our two children Sarah and Jonathan for their support and encouragement, without which this book could never have been completed.

If you enjoyed *A Brand To Die For*, you may care to leave a review on Amazon and Goodreads. Doing so will help give the book greater exposure.

Thank you.

ALEX PEARL

Sleeping with the Blackbirds

"A delightful fairy story
that deals sensitively and
compellingly with
real, modern-day issues like
homelessness, single mums
and abusive parents."

George Layton, actor,
screenwriter and author of
bestsellers, 'The Trick',
'The Swap' and 'The Fib'.

"A delightful fairy story that deals sensitively and compellingly with real, modern-day issues like homelessness, single mums and abusive parents."
George Layton, actor, screenwriter and author

"What an entrancing story. A real flight of fancy, which will engage children in the plot and, at the same time, increase their understanding of real human relationships."
Hugh Salmon, playwright and co-founder of Lovereading.co.uk

"Wonderful images and thought-provoking scenes."
Bramwell Tovey, composer & broadcaster

"The strength of the author's voice held me captivated long after turning the last page. With the wit of JK Rowling, Alex Pearl has definitely earned his place in the young adult fiction hall of fame."
Lisa McCombs, Readers' Favorite

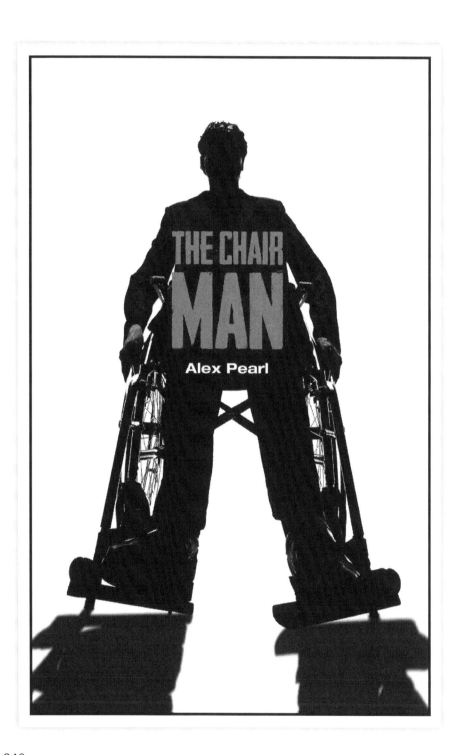

"More than a touch of John le Carré in this. All aspects of it are incredibly well researched for a start - it truly feels like the author comes from the world of espionage and knows what he's talking about."
Grant Price, author of By the Feet of Men

"As a big fan of police dramas like Line of Duty, I love a good twist at the end and this story doesn't disappoint."
Simon Pinnell, Forward magazine

"What really sells this story is the meticulous attention to detail, both in researching the facts of that fateful day and how terrorist cells operate, but Alex Pearl also goes into incredible detail when he's making stuff up, and that's why it can sometimes be hard to tell where fact ends and fiction begins, and I loved that!"
Philip Henry, author of the North Coast Bloodlines series

100 WAYS TO WRITE A BOOK

100 AUTHORS IN CONVERSATION WITH ALEX PEARL ABOUT THEIR BACKGROUNDS, MOTIVATIONS AND WORKING METHODS

"I was really chuffed to be asked to contribute to this fantastic project, and I wish I'd had this book on my bookshelf not just when I was starting out as a writer but throughout my career. There is so much wisdom here, I'd consider it essential for new and established writers alike. I also love dipping into it and being surprised by how authors reveal themselves in their conversations with Alex. The variety of tips on how authors market their books alone is worth the book's (considerable!) weight. This is a terrific companion for everyone who writes. The fact that any proceeds from the book will be donated to Pen Int'l (an incredible organisation that does fantastic work globally for writers in dreadful regimes) is commendable."

C. J. Carver, author of 15 acclaimed novels

"This is a fascinating insight into the process of writing and proves that all writers share one thing in common - they are all different! Much to be recommended."

John Dean, former journalist and acclaimed crime writer

"All in all, the perfect book for any writer (or aspiring writer) - with the fundamental message shining through - You Are Not Alone!"

Simon Van Der Velde, author of the much-praised Backstories

Printed in Great Britain
by Amazon

86104850R00144